THE PAGODA DOCTORS

Sister Susanna Valentine was a treasure
—she ran the Pagoda Medical Centre in
Singapore with precision, everything neat
and under control. Then her life erupted
with the arrival of Dr Danny Redfearn.
This extrovert, unconventional man
threatened her haven of respectability and
she knew that life at the Pagoda would
never be the same again . . .

Lancashire born, Jenny Ashe read English at Birmingham, returning thence with a BA and RA—the latter being rheumatoid arthritis, which after barrels of various pills, and three operations, led to her becoming almost bionic, with two manmade joints. Married to a junior surgeon in Scotland, who was born in Malaysia, she returned to Liverpool with three Scottish children when her husband went into general practice in 1966. She has written non-stop after that—articles, short stories and radio talks. Her novels just had to be set in a medical environment, which she considers compassionate, fascinating and completely rewarding.

The Pagoda Doctors is Jenny Ashe's fifth Doctor-Nurse Romance.

THE PAGODA DOCTORS

BY
JENNY ASHE

To Mom

with all my love

Jenny Ashe

1986

MILLS & BOON LIMITED
15–16 BROOK'S MEWS
LONDON W1A 1DR

First published in Great Britain 1986 by Mills & Boon Limited

© Jenny Ashe 1986

Australian copyright 1986

ISBN 0 263 11162 8

Set in 10 on 11 pt Linotron Times
15–0586–56,500

Photoset by Rowland Phototypesetting Limited Bury St Edmunds, Suffolk Made and printed in Great Britain by Richard Clay (The Chaucer Press) Limited Bungay, Suffolk

CHAPTER ONE

WHEN the vivid sun was hidden behind the glistening white tower of the Gold Hill Plaza, Sister Susanna Valentine knew that they were halfway through the afternoon session. The white glare of the Singapore pavements outside cooled slightly, and a gentler light filtered into the leafy foyer of the Pagoda Medical Centre. The tinkling fountain by the large open glass doors glistened momentarily less brightly and Susanna methodically reached for the appointment book, to check, as she always did, that the doctors were keeping to time, and that everyone who was on the list had attended, and had been entered in the book of bills to be sent out.

The day had gone well. She didn't much care for patients who were late, or who were inconsiderate enough to stay longer than their allotted time. The sign on her desk said 'Sister Susanna Valentine— Administrator'—and she was proud of that. Being a good Theatre Sister was one thing, but being promoted to this exalted post had done wonders for her self-confidence. She ran the Centre with precision, and when the Gold Hill Plaza hid the sun, the day was almost over, and she could congratulate herself on yet another trouble-free week.

Susanna ticked off the list neatly. She did everything neatly, from manicuring her antiseptic-fresh nails, to arranging the little lace cap in a geometrically perfect site on top of her clean blonde pleat of hair, where the individual hairs stayed perfectly in place, not daring to slip. She nodded in satisfaction. All patients had been on

5

time. Only two more women expected, both for Dr Roy
on the second floor. And three more for Dr Sovani, the
dental specialist, were already sitting quietly in his waiting area at the back of the ground floor, watching the
tropical fish, and the carefully tailored potted palms. Dr
Sovani had taken rather more notice of Susanna than
usual, and she looked with more than average interest at
his elegant white and gold door. He was definitely the
best-looking here. The nurses were all in love with him
and spent a lot of time gossiping when he was seen with a
new young lady. Susanna looked down again, and for
once her thoughts drifted away from her work . . .

'And who is Sister Susanna Valentine when she's at
home?'

It was an unexpected, unexplained male voice, and
Susanna looked up, already annoyed. The words were
impertinent—yet spoken in such a gentle, musical voice,
with a lilt of an accent she couldn't immediately place
—so that the sudden mention of her name sounded
almost like a caress, and made her aware that it was quite
a lovely name after all.

She looked up into a sea-green stare, a puckish face,
attractively creased in a gentle smile. Her own stare was
usually effective in reducing patients to a respectful
silence. But this pair of eyes, as deep, as green and
as unreadable as the ocean, disconcerted her. And
Susanna hated to be disconcerted. It reminded her that
her self-confidence so newly acquired was not yet fully
confirmed, and was capable of being knocked sideways.
But just by an impertinent male? Surely not?

He stood, tall, yet at ease, in blue denims and a dark
grey tee shirt. There was a canvas rucksack on his
shoulder, and he smiled again as he swung it down in
front of the desk. His hair was curly and dishevelled,
light brown, with perhaps a trace of silver at the temples.
So he could not be as boyish as he looked.

As icily as she could, Susanna said, 'Can I help you, sir?'

Softly, he said, 'Yes, Valentine dear. I've called to see Cissy Carlton. Is he in?'

Appalled, Susanna opened her mouth, and for a moment no words would come. She cleared her throat. '*Dr* Carlton has a patient with him. You have an appointment?' She knew he had not, but this did not disturb his easy manner. 'We cannot fit you in, I'm afraid. Not at this stage of the day.'

The man shook his head. 'I'm not after a consultation, Valentine. I'm a friend of his. Didn't he mention it? The name is Danny Redfearn, and I'm here to take a look at the suite you have to let.' He smiled again, creasing those attractive eyes so that they definitely twinkled at her. 'Top floor, Cissy said. Is it still vacant?'

Susanna could not help widening her eyes until they must have been almost round. 'You are a doctor?'

He looked down at her, and murmured, 'What gorgeous blue eyes.' Then he smiled at her expression, and went on, 'Yes, Valentine. Late of Guy's in London. You won't have heard of me, I expect. Neurologist.'

'Heard of you?' Something clicked in Susanna's memory. 'Oh, gosh. I mean—I think—er—you aren't Daniel T. Redfearn, are you? We have a book on laser treatment of spinal tumours.' But he didn't look like a writer, any more than he looked like a consultant neurologist. He reminded her more of an explorer—or a sports master—or a poet . . .

He looked pleased. 'The very same. Fancy Cissy buying my book.'

'Well, I chose it actually. We select from the publication lists three times a year. Mr Chan, our ENT surgeon, thought it would be interesting.'

'Then, Valentine, you are not only beautiful, you are an excellent administrator.' His smile was disarming

—but Susanna refused to be disarmed. She looked back at her appointment book, unsure what to say. Danny Redfearn watched her, and she was very conscious of his gaze, but she did not look up. He was too familiar, and she intended to show that she preferred a little more respect shown to her position here. While they waited, their silence was punctuated by the distant roar of city traffic, by the voices of passers-by, and occasionally by the high-pitched whine of young Dr Sovani's dental drill. The sun came out from behind the Gold Hill Plaza, and the foyer was again suddenly flooded with brightness.

Then, in his attractive accent, the famous neurologist who looked like a poet said gently, 'Well, Sister Valentine? Would you show me the suite that's for let? Or shall I make an appointment?' He was mocking her—but so lightly that she hardly realised it.

As he spoke, she recognised the lilting accent. 'Oh, I know. You're Irish.'

'Yes, indeed, Valentine. County Wicklow—though it's many a long year since I saw those gentle shores.' There was a world of meaning, of emotion, of experience in those few words. They were made more eloquent, as she looked up, by the gentle beauty of those eyes. She saw something in his face then, in the fine lines round his eyes and mouth, a long history of living and of suffering and overcoming—a life that Susanna had no notion of. He went on, with that smile coming back into his eyes, 'Don't you let rooms to Irishmen?'

Her self-assurance came back. 'Anyone who had the honour of meeting you, Dr Redfearn, would be happy to be able to help.' She stood up, and called to the office close by, 'Mei Li, I shall be upstairs. I'm showing the second floor suite to Dr Redfearn.' She reached for the drawer where she kept her keys.

Mei Li Tan stopped tapping on the electronic machine

in the corner of the airy office. 'Okay, Sue.' She appeared at the door, noticed Dr Redfearn, and smiled demurely, giving a little Chinese bow. 'Good afternoon, Dr Redfearn.' She came towards them, and Susanna noticed how Redfearn's eyes widened in appreciation of the graceful little figure, emphasised by the slim, high-necked cheongsam she wore.

'It is indeed, Mei Li.' Redfearn twinkled a while longer at her. Susanna was aware of the treatment—the man had a knack of making any female he spoke to feel that she was the only one in the world at that moment. She saw Mei Li's petal cheeks go pink, and knew how she felt. 'Will you be kind enough to look after this bag of mine?' He indicated the rucksack he had dumped on the floor. 'I'm sure I'll be only a moment. Cissy told me the rooms would be ideal for me.' And then another slow smile, taking in both girls, 'And I like the look of the ground floor a heck of a lot already.'

Susanna rattled the keys. 'This way, Doctor.' Her voice was businesslike. Pleasant though it was to be complimented, she felt her authority threatened. The Pagoda Medical Centre was not the place for such trifling. None of the other doctors dared to flirt so openly. The arrival of this astonishing man could be very disruptive if she were not very careful. The sooner he saw how things were done here, the better. 'The two theatres are on this floor, and a physiotherapy area. The rest of the floor is the Dental Department, run by Dr Sovani. That is his waiting room over there.'

Redfearn followed her towards the lifts. 'And Cissy is on the next floor, he told me.'

'Dr Carlton, yes. And Mr Chan, the ENT surgeon, and the anaesthetist, Dr Chou.' They were swishing up in the air-conditioned lift, and Susanna kept her eyes firmly on the lights flashing the floors. She knew that Dr Redfearn was once again appraising her figure, and tried

not to be self-conscious about her neatly pressed uniform and silver-buckled belt. None of the other doctors
looked at her like that.

'You call him Doctor, then, and not C.C.? That's very
formal, for a group working together. I'd like you to call
me Danny.'

Susanna pressed her lips together, before relying
primly, 'All right, I'll remember.'

Redfearn stood back to let her out on the second floor.
'This is mine, then, is it?'

'This is Suite Six. Dr Roy has Suite Five down the
corridor.'

'It's well set up, Valentine, I must say. Belongs to a Mr
Paw, I believe. What's he like?'

'Businesslike—fair. We have a good arrangement.
He believes in giving good value for good money.'

'So do I. Am I down here?' He set off without waiting
for her, with a long, lithe stride. Susanna followed,
trying not to admire his physique, which ought to have
been well-disguised by a business shirt and tie, instead of
being so obvious in a close fitting tee shirt and jeans.

He was delighted by the suite of consulting rooms. It
was decorated in shades of coffee and cream, with a few
vermilion scatter-cushions in the waiting area. There
was a vase with scarlet bird-of-paradise flowers too, and
the place was impeccably clean, the surface shining.
Susanna prided herself on keeping the cleaners up to
standard.

'I'll take it.'

He hadn't been in the place more than a minute.
'Aren't you being a bit impulsive?' Susanna asked.

He smiled down at her, and she found herself conned
into smiling back. 'I don't believe in hanging about when
my mind is made up, Valentine. I don't mind starting at
once. I could sleep on the couch, then, and it would save
finding a hotel for tonight.'

She felt suddenly sorry for him. 'You mean you—just arrived?'

'Flew in from London an hour ago.'

It all seemed terribly irregular. He was far too non-conformist for the Pagoda. Anyone else would have fixed up accommodation first. She found herself saying, 'You are more like a student than a consultant.'

He sat down at the elegant desk, and tipped the chair back on to two legs, smiling up at her, his green eyes vivid in the late afternoon sunshine that streamed in through the venetian blinds. 'No, Valentine. The difference is that students are haphazard about things. But my lack of dignity is carefully cultivated. I can't abide stuffy people.'

Susanna felt a stab in her heart, although the charming man opposite had not implied that she was stuffy. Or had he? She felt threatened again. 'But there is quite a distinction between stuffy and dignified.'

'I heartily agree with you, Valentine. And real dignity needs no false airs and graces. It is dignity of spirit, of soul. Nothing can hide that.'

He was undermining everything she believed in. This conversation had to stop. If only Danny Redfearn had not walked into the Pagoda while the sun was behind the Gold Hill Plaza. However, he was here, and obviously intending and willing to pay good money for Suite Six. That much was good news, for the owner, Augustus Paw and his lady wife worshipped at the shrine of Profit, and had been asking Susanna every time she settled the accounts, when she was going to let the last suite.

In fact, so unsure of him did she feel, that Susanna would have gladly lied, and told Redfearn that the suite was no longer available, if she had no-one but herself to answer to. But when he smilingly asked, in that fascinating drawl, 'Have we a deal, Valentine?', she knew she had no alternative but to assent. He held out his hand.

As she took it, he rose from the chair and said graciously, 'Probably the loveliest landlady in the country.'

She frowned slightly. 'I must get back downstairs. Mei Li might need me.'

'Rightie.' He went to the door, and held it open for her. 'But I discern, Valentine, that it is you who might need Mei Li. You are very much in control here, aren't you, Valentine? You like to know what is going on. You have a tidy little world here, and, like a dragon spider, you sit at the centre of your web and monitor everyone.' They had locked the door, and were walking towards the lifts, when he murmured, 'Watch it, Valentine. You may grow up to be one of those Gorgons who terrorise young housemen at nights, and give their nurses hell for wearing a pink hair ribbon instead of a white one.'

She pressed the button for Ground floor, saying nothing. This man had said enough for both of them that afternoon. But he had raised a strange apprehension in her in the few short minutes of their acquaintance. Suppose everything he said were true? He certainly spoke with an assurance that went with his years. How old was he? Thirty-five? Forty? He looked like a boy, yet addressed a woman like a man—a man who knew women and knew how to demolish their defences . . .

The lift swished to a stop and the doors opened. Neither of them moved for a moment. Then he said, 'I'm sorry, Valentine. I didn't mean to upset you.'

She turned to him. 'But you haven't,' she began —then she saw the look in the green eyes, and knew she had given herself away.

'I'll make it up,' he promised.

It was nearly five by now. Susanna went into the office and brought out the agreement of terms for him to sign. Mei Li witnessed their signature, and Susanna handed over the keys, and a copy of the agreement. 'Welcome to the Pagoda, Dr Redfearn.'

She knew she was blushing. She knew she was unhappy at the agreement, and wished that Danny
Redfearn had not stayed. So it was with tremendous
relief she saw Gerry Sovani walk down the passage to the
foyer, to see out his last patient. He was tall and slim,
and so gracefully did he walk on that deep pile carpet
that his feet left no trace. Susanna knew that part of his
attraction to her was the perfect neatness and good taste
of his clothes. He never bought a shirt alone. He always
bought an outfit, always hand-tailored, and each with
every detail in tune, from the diamond cuff-links to the
neat tie, the matching socks, and the polished shoes. His
hair, like hers, was never out of place, and gleamed with
a healthy blue-black, neither too short nor too long. His
black eyes were kind, yet aristocratic. In fact, together
with his gentle voice and excellent manners, there was
nothing about Gerry you could fail to like. The only
problem, from Susanna's point of view, was that he was
too popular. He managed to take out a different girl
every week, each one lovelier and more glamorous than
the last. His nurses idolised him, and vied with each
other to be prettier, better made-up, and more polite.
Yet he was even-handed with them, showing no favours,
so that there was no jealousy among his staff, and no
ill-feeling.

The patient turned and shook hands with him on the
steps. The evening shadows were long across the white
pavements now, casting the shadows of the slim palms
outside, striping the ground with dappled sun. The
crowds were thicker, as rush hour began, and the traffic
noisier. And the savoury smells of a thousand food stalls
mingled with the sweetness of the evening flowers and
leaves, and the fumes from the taxis.

Sovani turned and walked towards the office, pulling
off his spotless white coat and handing it to Mei Li for the
laundry. He saw that Susanna was speaking to someone,

and he would have passed them with a polite bow, if she had not reached out her hand and said, 'Gerry, let me introduce you. This is Dr Daniel Redfearn, the—'

But Sovani already knew the name. He took the visitor's hand, and shook it warmly. 'This is an honour, sir. Your work is well-known to me and to my colleagues. Dr Carlton, of course, has told us a lot about you. And there is another ex-colleague of yours at the City Hospital. Do you recall Mr Macfarlane?'

'Indeed I do. Mac the Knife.' He turned to the girls, who were both registering shock and yet trying not to giggle at the term. 'Sorry, ladies. Forget you heard that.' He turned back to Gerry. 'It's an honour for me too, and I'd be obliged if you'd just call me Danny.'

Susanna explained quickly. 'Dr Redfearn is in Suite Six.'

'That is good news. And where are you staying, Danny?'

'I haven't decided yet. If poor old Cissy doesn't have a coronary when he sees me, I'm hoping he and Fenella can fit me in.'

Gerry smiled. 'I'm sure they'll be glad to. Their house is slightly larger than my small apartment. But you will be welcome there if you are stuck.'

The telephone purred politely on the desk, and Susanna excused herself to answer it. 'Sister, my patient ought to be admitted tomorrow. Mrs Singh. Her angina hasn't settled. She won't stay in now, so I've agreed for her to go home, and come back tomorrow. Call Ahmad, would you, with the limousine, and make sure he knows what time to pick her up in the morning.'

With customary precision, Susanna made the necessary notes in her book. 'Very well, Dr Carlton. Just for observation and rest?'

'Yes, please, my dear.' Carlton was one of the old school, with silvery hair and moustache, and a charming bedside manner. He had stayed in Singapore after the war, neither he nor his wife caring to exchange the sunny weather for the British rain. 'Her first name is Ratha, and she is fifty-three.'

'Fine. Yes, sir, I've got all that. And incidentally, Doctor, you have finished now, haven't you?'

'Yes, I'm on my way down.'

'I think I ought to warn you that an old friend of yours is here, from Guy's. Dr Redfearn has taken Suite Six.'

There was a minor explosion at the other end of the line, and the phone was banged down. Susanna smiled to herself, and looked across at Danny Redfearn. 'Dr Carlton is on the way, I think!'

'Good, good.' Redfearn seemed pleased. Then he looked back at the dentist. 'Go on, Gerry. If the apartment is vacant, then I'd like to look at it as soon as possible.'

'I'll have a word with Mr Cheung this evening.' Mr Cheung was Gerry's neighbour. So Danny Redfearn was moving into their block, which was only minutes away from the clinic. Susanna shook her head. There was clearly no way she could stop this happening. He would be working and living here now. No escape from his cheerful words, his gentle phrases that did nothing at all but make her feel very uncomfortable. Perhaps, once he was working, she would find that he annoyed her less. Well, they had to give it a try.

The doctors usually met in the office, which was large enough and comfortable enough to double as a lounge. When there were more than three finished, Susanna usually rang one of the maids for tea. So when Carlton appeared at the door to greet his old friend with great pleasure, she went to him to take the tape of his letters for Mei Li to type, then rang the bell. 'Any letters for now, sir?'

'No. They'll all do tomorrow. But I want to go along

to the ward to see the diabetic laddie, and the old soul with the belly-ache.'

'You'll have tea first?'

'Surely. How do you like your tea, Danny boy? You still prefer Darjeeling?'

'I do, if it's available.' The three men began a lively discussion about the present state of the profession, and Danny was soon entertaining the others with stories of his past. Great shouts of laughter rose from their corner, while Susanna put away case sheets, and wondered what an important consultant was doing out here, with no strings, wandering like a student or a hippie. Most consultants at his age would be deep in their work, with a brood of children to educate. And with his charm, it would be unlikely for him not to be married. Divorced? Somehow it didn't fit.

He glanced across in the middle of a story, and caught her looking at him. A smile came to his eyes and he gave her a surreptitious wink, before turning back to the conversation. She felt a blush colour her cheeks. As she herself turned away, she knew the Pagoda would never be the same again, never be what it had been to her, a safe haven of respectability, a secure and well-ordered setting for the pearl of Susanna's organisation and skilful administration. There was a streak of anger and irritation in the way she closed the drawers of the filing cabinets with a sudden slam.

Dr Roy was next to finish. He handed his tape to Mei Li and took his tea from the tray with a courteous acknowledgement. The surgeon and anaesthetist from the first floor were last down. Mr Chan and Mr Chou were good friends, and also the jolliest of the group, always cheerful and ready for a gossip or a joke.

Phil Chan was fiftyish, balding but dapper. He made no secret of his delight at their new partner. 'So, sir, don't forget, your department starts here—' he placed his hands just above his spectacles, in a line from eye-brows to ears. 'Anything below that is mine.'

'Believe me, I don't want anything to do with your old ears. They are far too complicated for me. Give me a nice straightforward brain every time.'

Dr Chou, usually called Jo-Jo, was small and what Mei Li called 'cuddly'. He was a sunny-tempered man, friendly and never put out. 'Your arrival calls for a celebration. Why don't I take you over to the Plaza for a drink?'

Even Danny realised that he was not dressed for a smart club. But Dr Carlton had a better idea. 'Now, Danny, you'll be staying with me until you are fixed up. Why don't you all join us tomorrow night for a welcome dinner? I mean, the poor man must be jet-lagged to the eyeballs. Just see how weary he looks!' There was more good-humoured laughter at that, for Danny Redfearn looked as though he was just beginning to enjoy himself. Carlton turned to Susanna, who was busy making sure that Mei Li had all the tapes ready for tomorrow, and all the white coats were collected for the laundry. Ahmad had just brought the limousine to the front door, and Dr Carlton's nurse, Jackie, was helping little Mrs Singh out to the car. 'Sister Valentine, I hope you will come too.'

She looked up. There was nothing but pleasure and comradeship on the faces of the Pagoda doctors. Didn't they feel threatened by this extrovert and unconvention-al man, as she did? They treated him as an honoured guest. They delighted in his arrival. How could they? But an invitation from Dr Carlton was an honour too. 'Thank you, Doctor.' Her tone was suitably grateful. After all, she was included with the top brass, the sharp end of the management, not the nurses and secretaries. That had to be a plus. But it was going to expose her to extra hassles, of that she was sure.

The doctors drifted away, two to do a ward round, and
the others out of the clinic, into the Singapore twilight,
the middle-world of twinkling stars and twinkling neon
signs, of tiredness at the end of a weary day, and
alertness, as the lucky ones emerged in search of enter-
tainment and delight. Susanna locked her desk and gave
the keys to the doorman, Rahman.

'I say, Sue, what an attractive man.' It was Mei Li,
ready to go home, with her shoulder bag and her high-
heeled sandals, but wanting to talk a little. 'What a
fascinating life he must have had, can't you sense it? He
is so much more interesting than just being handsome.
He has that wonderful sophisticated air of having seen it
all before. Can't you see what a challenge it is, getting
someone like that to take some notice of you? After all
the hundreds of women he must have known?' She
sighed, half in jest, but with a ring of sincerity too.

The two dental nurses had stopped to dump their
white coats in the laundry basket. 'I know what you
mean, Mei Li. I saw the way he spoke to you, as though
nothing else in the world mattered.'

Susanna snorted. 'Don't act like schoolgirls with a
crush on a teacher. He just happens to have perfected a
line, that's all. Uses it on anything in skirts. I think it's
pathetic. And annoying.'

'What's annoying, Valentine?'

'Oh—' Susanna caught her breath, as Danny Redfearn came striding back into the foyer.

He smiled, and the depth of those sea-green eyes was
directed full at her. 'I came to pick up my rucksack. Oh,
thank you, Mei Li. Good girl. See you tomorrow, then,
Valentine.'

Her heart somersaulted. 'Yes, I expect so.'

He lowered his voice to a stage whisper. 'And I'll
promise to wear a tie and wash behind my ears.' The
other girls giggled. He was getting at Susanna in front of

them, and she felt mortified. There was no need to make fun of her, just because she was tidy and methodical. She was saved by the gentle purr of the telephone. Redfearn waved and went off, and the other girls bunched up in twos and threes on their way home.

'Hello? Pagoda?' she said.

'Ellen Paw here, Susanna. Have you got the week's receipts?'

'Yes, Mrs Paw.' Her employer's wife was a dumpy little lady, with owl-like spectacles and a calculator for a brain.

'That's fine. Shall I pick them up now?'

'Certainly. I'll leave them in the safe.'

'Thank you, dear. There is just one more thing. My daughter is back—you know she has just graduated from the London Business School?'

'I didn't know. Congratulations.'

'I'd like you to take her on for a month or so as a temp. She ought to see how the employee feels. Would that be convenient?'

Of course it would—how could anyone say no to their employer? 'That would be very nice, Mrs Paw.'

'Good. You'll meet her at the Carltons' tomorrow night, and she can start on Monday, the same time as the new doctor. You've signed the papers with Dr Redfearn, I take it?'

'Yes, Mrs Paw. They're here for you to see when you call.'

'Good girl, well done. You are a treasure, Susanna. I know you will get on well with Tilly. See you tomorrow, then.'

When Susanna left the Pagoda, it was as neat and uncluttered as on the day it opened. Even yesterday's magazines were tidied away, and the tables smelling of polish, waiting for the new ones on Monday. Yes, she had to agree with Ellen Paw. She was quite a treasure

—good at her job, and efficient. No one had any complaints about Susanna—except Danny Redfearn, who thought she was a dragon spider who frightened housemen and student nurses.

She looked back at the Chinese style portico, with its ornamental curved roof, and stone lions on each side of the now closed doors. There was a strong smell of joss sticks from the temple down the road, and some tinkling Chinese music from a transistor through someone's upstairs window. And into this neat, this orderly and cultured environment, a man had charged with all the impact of a herd of water buffalo. A man who didn't fit in. A man with eyes that reminded her of the sea . . . beautiful but treacherous.

CHAPTER TWO

In the crowded little island that was Singapore, a house with a garden was quite a luxury. Susanna, like most people, lived in an apartment block and relied for a garden on the spacious parks, Botanic Gardens, and the masses of flowers and shrubs that lined most roads. But the Carltons had a garden, and the Saturday night party was to be held there. Susanna had been on several occasions and knew Mrs Carlton, Fenella to her friends, and also the two Carlton girls, both now away at University. So why on earth was she taking so long to decide what to wear?

Mei Li had called in during the afternoon, as she often did when she went to the Plaza shops, because Susanna was handy in the next block. The two girls would go to the Silver Swan bar, where the tables spilled out in reckless abandon across the spotless pavements, and order ice-cream sodas in tall glasses, beaded with condensation under the spreading palm trees.

'You go to the Carltons' tonight?'

Susanna sighed. 'I do.' She toyed with her long stemmed glass, tracing a line through the condensation round the rim.

Mei Li laughed, a light bubbling laugh. 'Oh, Sue, don't look as though it is a funeral. Gerry Sovani will be there, remember.' There was mischief in the almond eyes. She had noticed the usually staid Susanna gazing absently at Sovani's white and gold door, listening to the whine of his drill as though it had been sweet music. 'Susanna, smile, for goodness sake? You know he treats us all the same when we're at work. Now is your chance

21

to see if he is more attentive in private.'

'Private? With all the doctors and their wives, plus the Paw family? He'll probably be just the same—polite, considerate—but nothing more, Mei Li, you must realise that the poor man is hounded by females. The last thing he'd want to do would be to chase *them*.'

'But aren't you different? You are just as aloof and courteous as he is, don't you see?' Mei Li took a long and inelegant swig of her soda through the pink straw. 'Made for each other,' she decided, sitting back, and smoothing her white jeans where the ice-cream had spilt. 'What will you wear?'

Susanna frowned. 'That's the whole point. I've no idea. I put out my white pleated skirt and dark blue silk blouse. But all of a sudden it looked just like a school uniform, not partyish at all. And I spend every day in uniform. It seemed wrong.'

'But it suits you.'

'It suits—the nurse in me. The side of me that wants everything neat and under control.' Now, why did she say that? She knew all right, but hoped Mei Li wouldn't ask. 'There's more to me than that, I hope.'

Mei Li's giggle was infectious. 'Oh, Sue! Don't tell me you are a secret belly dancer in your spare time!'

Refusing to join in the laughter, Susanna said, 'If you must know, it's because that awful Dr Redfearn told me I would turn into a dragon. He more or less accused me of eating housemen alive for breakfast.'

'And you don't care what he thinks, do you?' teased Mei Li. 'A stranger in town, who walks in like Clint Eastwood with a rucksack on his back and ought to be called Chuck, or Hank, or Spike.'

Susanna allowed herself to smile then. 'Is that what you think? You could be right. Thanks, Mei Li. You've put him in his place all right.' She sipped at her melting ice-cream. Then she added dreamily, 'I rather like Clint Eastwood.'

'He's far too old for you.'

Susanna put down her glass. The words seemed to mean more than Mei Li had meant. Surely age didn't matter. A touch of silver in the hair—a hint of fine creases round the eye? Didn't it add to a man's attraction? She looked across at her friend, and decided not to say so. 'Well, I'm not wearing the white.'

'Then I can't advise you. I don't know what belly dancers wear when they put clothes on.'

Mei Li's good humour finally won the day, and Susanna found herself relaxing. 'After all, it's only a small party, not a presentation at Buckingham Palace,' she said.

'Have you ever seen Buckingham Palace, Sue?'

'Lots of times. I used to live in south London. I worked in Kent until I was qualified.'

'Why didn't you stay?'

Susanna smiled down at her empty glass. 'I think they call it itchy feet. I wanted to see the world. And when I saw Singapore, I never wanted to leave.'

'Your parents are there? In London?'

'Yes.' Susanna's thoughts flitted back to the day she had told the family what she wanted to do. They had immediately thought she was off white-slave trading, would get caught up in the drug scene, was far too young to take off on her own. . . . It hadn't been easy. It had taken guts, patience and a lot of tears. 'They might come out for a visit next year, when my brother goes to college.'

'Don't you miss them terribly?'

'I got used to being on my own when I was nursing. I think Mum was relieved when I left. We used to argue a lot. But yes, I do love them, and it will be nice to see them again.'

'They will be very proud of you,' Mei Li said.

'I suppose they will.' Sister Susanna Valentine—Administrator. Yes, she had done well, and she was happy. Or she had been until yesterday. Oh well, Dr Redfearn meant nothing. He said a lot of cheeky things —but it was only in fun. She wouldn't let him upset her at all. Not a jot. All the same—'Mei Li, do you remember that red chiffon dress I bought last year?'

'Oh yes—the little shift with tiny shoulder straps. Very sophisticated. You only wore it once.'

'Would it be over-dressed for tonight?'

'Certainly not. It would be great. Don't forget that the Paws' daughter will be there, straight from London. I bet she's wearing something that costs the earth. Yes, Sue, you have to show her that we're just as trendy as she is, right?'

'Agreed.' Susanna wondered if she would have dared to wear it, without that encouragement from Mei Li. But after mentioning it, she had to wear it—hadn't she?

When she was dressed and ready, Susanna had to admit that she liked what she saw in the mirror. Her slim neck and shoulders were tanned the colour of honey, shown off by the shoestring straps of the dress, and by the upswept pleat of white-gold hair, folded as neatly and perfectly as always. Her shoes were the same red as the dress. And for jewellery she chose silver drop ear-rings, and a heavy silver bangle above her elbow, leaving her neck bare.

The Carltons lived a short cab drive away from the city, out on the Bukit Timah Road. Their gardener fought a valiant battle against the rapidly growing foliage all round the garden. Round the lawn tall jack-fruit trees were laden with the heavy green gourds, and the mango tree was just beginning to produce small fruit. There were three banana trees at the back, shielding them from their neighbours, and helping to shield their guests from the last rays of the descending sun with their huge floppy leaves.

Drinks were out on small tables in the garden, and after greeting C.C. and Fenella Carlton, Susanna found herself in a small group with Phil Chan and his comfortable wife Goh Min. He was chatty, as usual, making no secret of his love of company. 'And headaches,' he was saying, 'Do you not see why I have so many grey hairs, Susanna? It is because of the patients with the headaches, no? There are a million causes for headaches.'

Mrs Chan smiled like a female Buddha. 'The reason you have grey hairs is because you are an old man, my dear.'

He pretended to be offended. 'Fifty? Old? Susanna, tell her.'

Susanna laughed, and sipped her white wine. 'Certainly not. I don't think you could ever be old. You never even seem tired, even when you operate all day. I don't think grey hair has much to do with it.' And then, as the friendly chatter continued, she suddenly saw Danny Redfearn come out of the bungalow, and recalled what she had said about the charm of older men. She blushed, and pretended she hadn't seen him.

She blushed again, as their group was augmented by the elegant figure of Gerry Sovani. Just as she was going to tell him how dashing he looked, in his carefully toning light grey trousers and silvery grey silk tailored shirt, he bent and said in her ear, 'Susanna, you look quite stunning tonight.'

Regaining composure, she said brightly, 'From you, that is a very genuine compliment. Some men wouldn't know about style if it stood up and crowed at them. You always look so smart.'

He basked in her words. 'I think it is important,' he

said, and his voice was attractively husky, with a slight
Indian accent. 'People tend to judge on appearances. It
may be wrong, but it happens, so I do not intend to be
misjudged.' He remembered the others, and asked Mrs
Chan, 'You think I am right, Goh Min? Please, be my
guest, and shout at me if you think I am wrong.'

'I daren't shout at my husband's favourite golf
partner, Gerry,' she laughed.

The crickets were getting noisier now, as night fell,
and the gardener switched on the strings of coloured
lights looped from tree to tree. Fenella Carlton came
round with a tray of savouries, closely followed by
Redfearn, a carved wooden bowl of prawn crackers in
each hand.

He handed them round, and gave Susanna a welcoming grin. 'My hostess has decided to keep both my hands
occupied, Valentine, so that I won't get into any mischief tonight.'

'Nonsense.' Fenella was a stout, hearty woman, with a
ready smile and a loud, mannish voice. 'The fellow
wanted to help. Susanna, if I were you I would make a
rule never to believe anything he says—it's all blarney.
He's a genius at it.'

'But you still love me, Fenny, don't you?'

'With all my heart, dear,' she said absently, looking
around her. Then she saw what she wanted. 'Suleiman,
come here. Take these bowls from this dreadful Irishman so that he can get himself a whisky.' The gardener
came over to assist her and Danny Redfearn used both
hands, as soon as they were free, to steer Susanna
away from the Chans, and over to a deserted corner
of the garden, under one of the spreading banana
trees.

'Stay,' he murmured.

'I'm not a dog,' countered Susanna, spiritedly.

'No, Valentine, but your glass is empty, and if you'll

hand it over, I'll bring us both one of my steamy tropical Specials.'

'You didn't think of asking if I'd like one first?'

He beamed, crinkling those eyes up in a face that reminded her of an angelic schoolboy caught at the cake-tin. 'You *will* like one.'

'How on earth can you be so sure of everything?'

'Practice.' And with a wave of the hand, he left her for a moment, to catch her breath. Before she could analyse her feelings, to find out if she was annoyed or excited at his cavalier treatment, he was back, with two crystal tumblers clinking with ice. He handed her one. 'To Valentine's Day.'

Susanna looked up at him, exasperated. 'To the first appearance of Dr Redfearn's tie.'

He grinned. 'You noticed. Well, I knew I had to live up to you, Valentine. You like it?' He was wearing a lightweight suit over a light green shirt, with a darker green tie.

'Yes, in fact, I have to say yes.' She sipped at the liquid, feeling it burn a pathway inside her. 'You nearly look like a doctor tonight.'

He paused, and studied her gravely for a moment. Again, when he gave her his full attention, she felt afraid, even though by moonlight it was impossible to see the colour of his eyes properly. And suddenly they seemed terribly sad, deeply sad with an ocean of suffering. His voice seemed to come from far away, as he said softly, '*La Fille aux Cheveaux du Lin*. Do you know what that is, Valentine?'

Again, she felt afraid. How silly, when she was here, in the midst of friends and colleagues. 'Yes, I do. It's a piano piece by Debussy. I used to play it once, but I wasn't much good. The girl with flaxen hair.'

There was a hint of a smile on his lips, but his eyes were still sad. Susanna wondered if perhaps he had drunk more than it appeared of his tropical specials. When he spoke, it was as though she was no longer there. He was speaking to himself, thinking aloud. 'I used to play it too. I fell in love with that girl—used to see her in my mind when I played. She was slight, and cheerful. Her hair—it was exactly the same colour as yours, Valentine, but it needed cutting, and it streamed behind her when she ran. And she had sand on her bare legs, and a splash of mud on her loose white cotton dress. She had freckles on her nose, and she carried a bunch of wild flowers . . .' He stopped, and his eyes came back to the present. 'Sorry. My imagination again.' He cleared his throat.

Susanna knew she had to speak. But the only words she could find were prosaic ones. She was acutely conscious of her own neatness—suddenly it seemed terribly out of place. 'Have you found somewhere to live yet?'

He leaned back against the trunk of the banana tree, and smiled ruefully, as though he might have known she couldn't accompany him to the heights of his imagination. 'I think I've got that apartment in Gerry's place. It'll be handy for work. I'll start on Monday morning, even though I have no appointments yet, if that's okay with you?'

'Yes, of course.'

And they both drank at the same time, as though words had run out, and there was nothing else to say.

Then Fenella was calling everyone to the table. It was a buffet supper, and Susanna was separated from Redfearn in the scramble for plates, forks and napkins. She took her plate to one side when she had collected enough cold meat and salad. And almost bumped into Ellen Paw, shimmering in a satin dress studded with sequins round the mandarin collar. 'Oh, how nice you look, Susanna. This is my daughter, Tilly.'

The girl standing beside Ellen Paw was one of the loveliest creatures Susanna had ever seen. She held her plate of food as though it were some divine vessel of the gods, and her dark hair streamed down loose, reminding Susanna of the girl with the flaxen hair, whom Danny had loved. Her small face was exquisite, with dark lustrous eyes, cheeks like peaches, and a small, smiling mouth. Chinese she may have been, but that face was perfection in any land. 'How nice to meet you.' There was scarcely a trace of accent. 'I too am from the UK. I have just finished a course at the Business School, after doing my Ph.D. in London.'

Susanna tried to sound natural. 'Well, it will be a pleasure to welcome you to the Pagoda on Monday, Tilly.'

Ellen Paw interrupted. 'You mustn't treat her any different from the others, Susanna. I want her to understand everyone's feelings, from the cleaning women to the directors.'

'Mother, I have done the course. There's no need to remind everyone. Naturally I must understand—that is the way to a happy and profitable company.'

Susanna couldn't help saying, 'You don't look like a tycoon yet, Tilly. I would have said you were still at school.'

'I'm twenty-eight.' The silvery voice hardened just a trifle. Susanna could tell by that, and by the mention of profit, that, fairy-like and dainty though she was, Tilly Paw was just a chip off the old block. Still, an extra typist was always useful.

Ellen Paw intervened again. 'Come and meet the new doctor, Tilly.' Redfearn was moving over in their direction, and Susanna stood back so that he and Tilly could come face to face. She recognised at once the look in his eyes. He looked at the Chinese beauty as though he couldn't take his eyes from her. She bowed gently,

sending out vibrations of politeness, of frailty and defer-
ence. Susanna noticed that when she spoke, she made no
reference to the doctor of her skill and cleverness. She
was a clever girl, all right. The neurologist was already
smitten. Susanna knew that Tilly would brook no competition. The only thing was, that the little hussy would
never be satisfied with a mere doctor. She would settle
for nothing less than a millionaire. And Danny would be
hurt . . .

She made an excuse, and moved away. The evening
was hot and stuffy. It would have been cooler indoors,
but chairs were out on the verandah, and Fenella clearly
wanted her guests to stay outside. Susanna sat down next
to Jo-Jo, who was resting between courses, drinking
white wine and fanning himself with a folded napkin.
'Have you met Tilly?'

Jo-Jo nodded and smiled. 'Competition, Susie?' He
and Phil made jokes that no-one ever minded.

Susanna said lightly, 'Not really. I'm the Administrator, remember. No-one gets out of line when I'm
around.'

Jo-Jo's elfin face crinkled in another smile. 'The battle
of the Titans.'

'You surely don't think that two respectable girls can't
work together without quarrelling?' Susanna was only
half serious.

Shaking his head wisely, Jo-Jo said, 'They can work
together till kingdom-come, so long as there isn't a man
involved.'

Susanna lifted her chin. 'Then there's no problem, is
there? Tilly is only in love with money, and I with my
work.'

There was a shrill cry, as a jay swooped across the
garden. The crickets were chirping so loudly that their
sound had become invisible. Someone put a tape on in
the house, and Dr Carlton went across to invite Ellen

Paw to dance. Gradually they were joined by others. It was gentle, romantic music, and Susanna was happy when Gerry Sovani asked her. She stood up, and was held firmly and close by Gerry's strong hand. She enjoyed the sensation of moving closely with someone as handsome, as tall and eye-catching. He moved his hand slightly on her back, and she found herself feeling slightly breathless and trembly.

'You don't dance for pleasure, Sue?' His voice was low, as he bent so that their cheeks were almost touching.

'Am I so bad?'

'You are perfect. You move with the music so beautifully.'

She had to remember that this man was experienced with women. It was no use trying to think of anything smart to say. He would have heard it all before. 'Since coming to Singapore, I've not done very much for pleasure. I worked quite hard for the first couple of years. Now that I know my job, I find that the cinema, or a meal out with Mei Li, is all I do in my spare time.'

'You've no boyfriends, then?'

'Nothing intense.' She kept her tone light. In fact, she had always ducked away from anything intense. She liked to be the one in charge of a situation. Falling in love must be a helpless feeling, and it frightened her. 'Why the sudden interest, Gerry?'

'Well, perhaps it isn't all that sudden. How would you know?'

'Don't fool me. I've seen you with so many girls in the last three years that I've lost count.'

He held her a trifle closer, and she didn't resist. The feeling of his strong young body, hard and vibrant, was tonight more acceptable to her than yesterday. Perhaps there was nothing wrong with a little intensity, if it were

with someone she admired—and if it didn't trap her
mind and soul as well as her body.

'Susanna,' Gerry said. 'My dear, how will we know
who we get on with, if we don't have others to compare
with?'

'What a good argument. Congratulations, Gerry.
Now I know why you've got all those letters after your
name.'

'Don't tease me.' That must be another of his lines.
But there was no doubt but that it made an impact. She
felt immediately motherly, protective. 'You know that
women frighten me?'

'Then why didn't you marry the girl your parents
chose for you?'

'Susanna! How did you know that?'

'Go on dancing, Gerry. It's no magic. Only Indian and
Chinese parents still like to think that their children take
notice of what they advise. If I've learnt nothing else
since I've been in Singapore, I know that.'

'It has proved pretty successful in the past.'

'So, answer my question—why didn't you?'

Gerry had a slow smile that started in his deep black
eyes, then turned the corners of his mouth up, finally
showing a set of perfect white teeth that shone in his
darkly handsome face. 'Arranged marriages are all very
well—a proportion of them turn out wonderfully—but I
have a feeling that when things get rough in a marriage
—and they do, even in the best households—then I
think there is a need for something deeper. Do you know
what I mean?'

'I think so. In the middle of an argument, two people
might get very angry, and say bad things. But if they
have a shared mutual affection, they get over this, and
the others don't. Is that what you mean?'

'I can't prove it. But yes, that's my gut feeling. Love is
a foolish word. People make it mean anything they want.

But I'm still looking for it.' They had stopped dancing while they talked, but still stood, his arm around her waist, at the end of the verandah, looking into each other's eyes. 'Do you think I'm crying for the moon?'

Susanna was subdued. 'I've never really thought about it. But no. If you want something, then keep looking.' She added suddenly, 'I must say it's better to search for love than to search for money. I get pretty tired of people who measure success by the length of your limousine.'

'Well—' Gerry smiled again, rather shamefaced, 'I do have a Mercedes as well. But it's nice to hear you understand what I'm trying to say. Perhaps we could have dinner sometime?'

There. He had said it. Mei Li had bet her he would. And Susanna felt suddenly ashamed, to bet on something that was really not a joking matter. 'Thank you, Gerry.'

They were startled by the clapping of hands. Fenella Carlton was calling, in her contralto tones, 'Quiet a moment, everyone.'

Then her husband came forward, and in each hand he held up a green frosted bottle of chilled champagne. 'Ladies and Gentlemen, I hope you haven't forgotten that this is a "Welcome to the Pagoda" party. Come here, Danny, and let us all wish you a long and happy stay in Singapore, and much luck in the future.'

The guests clapped and cheered as Danny Redfearn walked slowly up the verandah steps. C.C. offered him a bottle. 'Open that, old man, while I have a go at this one.'

Danny took it, with a modest smile. 'I appreciate it, Cissy.' He turned to the others. 'Thank you all.' It was a small speech for an Irishman, but Susanna saw a look in his face that said a whole lot more. He levered the top from the bottle, and Fenella was close by with two glasses to catch the sparkling liquid. As she began to hand them out, it was just possible to hear Danny say *sotto voce* to C.C., 'I never saw anything that looked so like cerebro-spinal fluid.'

'I assure you it's not.' C.C. had tasted it. 'Here, my boy, wrap your tonsils round that.'

Danny did so, and nodded approval. He sat down beside his old friend, looking suddenly weary. He and Carlton were now the only ones on the verandah, apart from Susanna and Gerry who were at the far end. She could hear what they were saying, though the music had started up again. Carlton's voice was low. 'So—feel like talking, Danny? About Caroline? And about Sebastian?'

'Later, Cissy. Later tonight—if you can stand a whole lot of sob stuff.'

'You stood it,' said Carlton soberly.

'I had to.'

He tossed the last of the champagne down in one gulp, and stood up. Then a smile creased his eyes as he looked down into the lovely heart-shaped face of Tilly Paw. She smiled up at him, her legs bare, the loose cotton dress flowing in the welcome evening breeze. Her hair, too, floated like a dark cloud about her fairy face, and she held in one hand a white hibiscus flower.

Susanna made a sudden move. 'I think I ought to go home.'

'Already? Let's dance some more.'

But as Tilly stood looking up at Danny Redfearn, her hair touched with the silver of a moonbeam, she looked like some changeling elf child. And exactly like the imaginary love that Danny had described earlier. There was no need to look into his face. Susanna already knew where those sea-green eyes were gazing. And she turned away, feeling as though she were being squeezed out of a patch of magic, losing something precious that she had not yet had the chance of touching . . .

CHAPTER THREE

MEI LI TAN was hopping up and down when Susanna arrived for work on Monday morning. 'Tell me, Sue, tell me all about it. Did you look like a film star? I bet you did. What did the other women wear?'

Susanna walked briskly through to the changing room and hung up her street dress. While she buttoned her uniform, fastened the belt, and placed that lace cap in the exact centre of her head, she said cheerfully, 'Mei Li, be a dear and stop gossiping. I've got a thousand things to do, and Tilly Paw will be here any minute. Just you show her what the model secretary does with her morning.'

Mei Li grinned, deliberately annoying. 'Gosh, I've no idea. What does the ideal secretary do with her morning?' Her face was angelically innocent.

Susanna turned, satisfied with her own appearance. 'Sit at the typewriter, dear, and type letters. Now!' she added the last word rather loudly, and Mei Li jumped, and ran to the machine. 'I must remember to find out which days Dr Redfearn wants to consult, so that I can give the order to the firm that does our brass plates.' And she went quickly to the desk, where she had a pad waiting for such notes, so that they were never forgotten.

Mei Li rolled a piece of paper into the typewriter. She typed the date. Then she looked around, and realised she hadn't arranged the tapes she had to type from. But when she glanced at Susanna, she saw with relief that her friend was smiling. Susanna pulled a face at her. She responded with a dignified, 'I'm sure I hope I give

36

satisfaction, ma'am.' At which both girls giggled, and Mei Li went on eagerly, 'At least you can tell me what Mrs Paw's daughter looks like.'

'I wish I didn't have to say this, but she is both beautiful and clever.'

Mei Li grinned. 'Don't worry, Sue. Men don't like clever women.'

'They do now. The government is encouraging clever women to marry and have clever children.'

'I don't care. It doesn't matter who tells them, men will still prefer women who make them feel good.'

Susanna smiled. 'You're not as dumb as you look. Right first time. And Tilly Paw has learned this very well. She's as bright as a button, but when talking to men—you'd think she wanted nothing but their personal happiness.' Susanna gasped then, as she saw the lovely form of Miss Paw tripping up the steps to the front door, with a bouquet of orchids in her arms. 'To your posts, men!'

Mei Li read the signal, and demurely turned to her machine, fitting one of the tapes to her audio receiver.

Tilly was wearing a plain grey skirt and a white blouse. However, as she was one of nature's beauties, it didn't matter what she wore—she captivated any watchers. 'Hello, Susanna. I've brought some flowers for your desk.' Her lovely hair was swept into a chignon, pinned with pearls.

'That is kind.' Susanna accepted them with a brilliant smile, then she handed them over to Mei Li, who jumped up to take them. 'But I feel that there are enough flowers in the foyer, so I try to keep my desk more—business-like, if you see what I mean.'

Tilly smiled, her oriental eyes giving nothing away. 'How very sensible. I must remember that.' She sauntered up to the desk slowly. 'Now, do give me lots of orders, Susanna.'

Susanna hid a smile. Ellen Paw had told her to treat Tilly as just another employee. But how could she? She said sweetly, 'Tilly, I think you ought to see around the place first. It won't be easy, unless you know where everything is.'

'Oh, but I do, dear. Mother gave me a plan. I'm quite familiar with the workings of the Centre.'

Susanna took a deep breath. This was going to be just as hard as she had anticipated, and she had to show this woman that she was the boss. Nothing was going to upset her schedule. It had worked like clockwork since she took over. One good-looking debutante wasn't going to put her pretty spanner into anyone's works. 'Very well, dear.' She used the familiarity, even though she knew that Tilly was older than she was. It helped to preserve her own image to herself. 'Then perhaps you wouldn't mind giving out the mail.'

'Certainly, Sue.' Tilly was quick to counter the familiarity. She took the handful of letters that Susanna offered. 'Dr Roy and Dr Redfearn upstairs, Dr Chou and Mr Chan on the middle floor, with Dr Carlton at the front. All dental matters to be handed to Amanda, Dr Sovani's receptionist.' She smiled sweetly.

At that moment, Gerry himself arrived, moving elegantly through the open doors, his head high, the morning sun shining on his impeccable hair. Susanna felt a sense of pride, that such a perfect human being should belong to their establishment. He turned female heads wherever he went, and Tilly Paw, she noticed, was no exception. She made for Gerry with a charming smile, greeting him daintily. 'I have some mail for you. Shall I come in with it?' Susanna bit her lip to stop herself smiling. Gerry hated to be rushed. He liked to sit in his own office, drink a cup of green tea, and then read his mail, before donning his white coat, freshly hung in his surgery each morning.

But to her chagrin, Gerry didn't seem to mind at all. It was Amanda, the receptionist, whose face turned hard with annoyance at the intrusion of Miss Paw into her private little domain. Somehow, a great deal of tact would be needed, so long as Tilly remained. And Tilly might just decide that working for six men was more fun than running her own empire in a lonely office. Susanna turned back to answer the telephone. She must let things sort themselves out.

The voice on the phone sounded fraught. 'Pagoda? Thank goodness. I've been told that you have a Dr Redfearn there, the famous neurologist?'

'That is right. He will be in this morning.'

'Oh, that's wonderful. May I see him, please?'

The woman was on the point of tears. Susanna said soothingly, 'Yes, of course. Would it suit you to come in an hour?'

'No earlier appointment?'

'Well, you could come and wait for him if you like. Is it very urgent? Is there anything I can do? If you need a doctor urgently, you should go to the City, you know.'

'No, no. I'll come and wait. Thank you very much. My name is Ming.'

'Very well, Mrs Ming. I'll put your name down.'

It was surprising that Redfearn had a client so soon. His name was not yet on the board at the door, and his arrival had been a suprise to even his best friend. Susanna puzzled, but not for long, for there was far too much to do.

'Good morning, Valentine.'

She looked up. 'Good morning, Dr Redfearn. I didn't expect you so early.'

He gave her a sideways look. 'Sure, you've got a terrible bad image of me, my dear. I bet you thought I'd turn up in jeans too.' He was in dark grey slacks, a white shirt and a dark red tie. His shoes were polished, and his hair was sleeked back, and parted on one side. Though even that treatment didn't prevent a couple of brown curls from breaking out, making him look attractively young.

She swallowed her pride. 'I apologise. I expect I really did look a bit disapproving when you walked in last Friday. My face was probably worse than my bite.'

He grinned, and said, 'Your bite was quite severe too.'

She grinned back at that. 'Then I'm afraid I'll just have to accept that I'm a dragon after all.'

He lifted one well-shaped hand in protest. 'No, no, dear, not yet. No one as gorgeous as you could be that. Wait till you've lost your looks, though, then, remember what Uncle Danny forecast.'

Smiling, she pulled out the appointment book. 'To work, sir. I'm afraid you have a patient—even before I've had time to write your name in the book.'

'That's very odd. How did they know?'

'No idea. It's a Mrs Ming, and she's on the way now. You'd better ask her yourself.'

'Okay, will do.'

'There'll be a white coat in your room. The nurse on your floor is Raya, and she'll order a cup of tea or coffee if you want one. Darjeeling, isn't it?'

'Good lord, you even noted that. Thanks, Valentine.' He gave her a wink, and strode off towards the lifts. Susanna went back to her work. Dr Roy and Dr Carlton were the only two others to come in today. But she knew that Phil Chan would pop in, to make sure his tonsillectomy of last week was still progressing normally.

Mrs Ming arrived in a taxi only moments later. She was a tall, quite elegant Chinese lady, well-dressed in a linen skirt and top in pale blue. But her face was tense with worry, the eyes showed signs of weeping, and the lips were pressed tightly together. Thank goodness

Danny had arrived, Susanna thought. 'This way, Mrs Ming. I'll take you straight up. Mr Redfearn is here.'

A musical voice interrupted. 'Susanna, let me save you the trouble.' Tilly was back. 'I can take the lady up for you. I've done the letters.'

'Right. Thank you.' Susanna turned back to her desk, and tried not to be annoyed at Tilly interfering. She probably wanted to chat to Danny. She clearly didn't think twice about the problem the patient might be having. Susanna wondered whether it was worth while explaining this to her. It could be vital. The patient's interests must always come first.

She was busy getting out records of the patients to be seen by the other two doctors that afternoon, when the buzzer sounded urgently. She picked up the phone quickly. 'Yes?'

'Valentine.' It was Redfearn, obviously. No one else called her that. 'Mrs Ming—where does she live? Has she a phone number?'

'No. She was in a hurry to see you, so I sent her straight up.'

'Oh, God, I didn't realise. Tilly didn't tell me. Val, she's fitting. Raya is with her, but I'll have to admit her right away. Is that all right?'

'Yes, of course. I'll get the trolley there at once.'

'And you've no idea where she lives?'

Susanna thought quickly. 'Well, she didn't take long to get here after telephoning me, so it can't be far out. I'll go through the phone book. There must be hundreds of Mings, but I could check the ones who live within a short distance of here.'

'Good girl. Thanks.' The receiver was down almost before he had said the last word. Susanna looked around angrily. Where was Tilly? She had kept Danny in ignorance of the fact that he had an emergency on his hands. Probably flirting with him! Tilly Paw had certainly not

made a very good impression on her first day. Anyone
else would have been reprimanded at once. Susanna
hesitated to do so in this case. She would give her one
more chance, and try to explain tactfully what she had
done wrong. It wouldn't be easy. Here was a woman
with a serious convulsion. Nothing could be done until
they found out who she was, what relatives she had, and
whether she had a history of fits. Susanna frowned. She
had been partly to blame. She usually took the address
as soon as new patients booked in. She had left it in Mrs
Ming's case, as she had looked so ill and worried. She
was at fault too.

'Susanna, my diabetic boy can be discharged this
morning.'

'Right, Dr Carlton. I'll contact his home.'

'Give me a buzz when he's going.'

'Yes sir.'

'You'll be in theatre in the morning, won't you?'

'Yes. Mei Li will be at the desk.'

'Good. Make sure there's a note to remind me to meet
my wife at eleven.'

'Yes, Dr Carlton.' Susanna made the note right away.
She hated forgetting anything, and was furious with
herself about Mrs Ming's address. But there was a
certain calmness in her mind at the same time. Tilly had
been annoying—and potentially negligent. She herself
had omitted to get information she ought to have got.
Yet they were small things—part of the job, almost.
Foolish to let small irritations assume too much import-
ance. Thank goodness lunchtime appeared, and the
doors were closed for a while.

'Okay, Sue, come and get it.' For the last eight or nine
months Susanna and Mei Li had decided not to go out
for a meal at lunchtime, but to spend the time in peaceful
relaxation, with only a snack of non-fattening salads and
tit-bits of fish and meat. Occasionally one would go out,

if there was any urgent shopping to do. But Susanna had suggested that one of them should always be near the phone. The answering machine was efficient, but she was conscious of the need for personal supervision—a machine cannot think, cannot interpret a frightened caller. So one of them always stayed.

'I'm coming. You aren't doing your yoga first, are you?'

'I've given that up for a while. It sent me to sleep at the wrong times.'

'Good.' Susanna sat on the carpet in the office, and leaned back against the wall, taking a large hunk of celery to chew on while they talked. 'You made me feel guilty, sitting here idle.'

Tilly Paw had been doing some typing. She had made a point of telling them how good her speed was, but Susanna merely replied that accuracy was much more important to their doctors. She now turned and handed the finished letters to Susanna. 'Well, headmistress?' Her pretty voice was cool and confident.

'Excellent, Tilly.' Even in her lunch hour, Susanna had jumped up, wiped her hands, and folded the letters before clipping them to their envelopes ready for signing. She slipped them neatly into the transparent folders. 'Would you like to join us for lunch? We don't usually go out. It's quite relaxing here, with the potted palms and the fountain.'

'And the tropical fish,' added Mei Li. 'And the air conditioning. It's too hot outside.'

'It is hot,' agreed Tilly, smoothing back her strands of dark hair that made her look waif-like and vulnerable —which she was certainly not. A look of cat-with-the-cream crept into her almond eyes, as she added, 'In fact, I'd love to stay here and chat with you. But I'm lunching with Dr Redfearn, and I promised to take him to one of Daddy's best restaurants.'

Mei Li tried not to open her mouth in surprise. 'Lucky old Redfearn.'

Susanna added darkly, 'Lucky old Tilly.'

Tilly said casually, 'I was quite surprised when he asked me. I had been rather naughty this morning, taking his mind off his work.' She gave a silvery laugh.

Susanna said, 'Well, as you've brought it up, you were a bit thoughtless. I meant to mention it later, but patients always come first here, no matter who they are. Idle chatter is for after hours only. But I'm sure you won't do it again.'

Tilly Paw didn't move a hair. She turned and looked out of the window through the slats in the venetian blind, and said quietly, 'Since we are mentioning faults, I noticed that you didn't say anything to six of the staff who arrived late, including myself. Not very efficient, that. And also you forgot to take the address and phone number of Dr Redfearn's patient, giving him endless extra trouble and worry.' She dropped the slats with a click, and turned round. 'Daddy will be interested to hear that, Susanna, I'm sure. Administrators are fairly easily replaced.'

'I—' Susanna's anger probably saved her. While she was trying to find the exact reply, Danny Redfearn appeared from the lift and crossed the floor jauntily. Tilly didn't allow him to get too near the office, but shot out to meet him and slipped her hand through the crook of his elbow. He waved at Susanna, and was gone, the door swinging behind them. She ran across, and shot the bolt in the main door. 'And don't come back,' she muttered, through clenched teeth.

Mei Li was waiting for her and as soon as she opened her mouth to let off steam, her mouth was stuffed with a large slice of mango. She had to keep quiet, or the juice would have run down her uniform. By the time she had successfully extricated herself from such a messy fate, her temper had cooled. 'Thanks, Mei Li.' They both sat down again, and sighed. 'It isn't easy. But it won't last forever. Her type always tire of things quickly and will want another toy from Daddy to play with.'

'I guess so. But if I had Danny Redfearn as a toy, I don't think I'd get tired. He's so—funny. I always wanted to meet a man who would make me laugh.'

Susanna didn't smile. 'I wanted to ask him about Mrs Ming. Mei Li, I think I'll just go out to the ward and ask Sister Silvano. When I phoned earlier, she was still sleeping, and hadn't said anything at all. I know I was wrong, not to ask her where she lived, but it seemed more important to get her medical help at the time.' And with her brow wrinkled with apprehension, she went over to rinse her hands and check her face for crumbs. 'All we can hope is that her family know where she is, and will contact us when she doesn't go home on time.'

She stood for a moment by the air-conditioning vent, enjoying the draught of cool air on her legs and body. Then she turned to go. At that moment there was a ring at the doorbell. 'Oh, bother.' They both looked across the foyer. A slim youth, with fair hair and an anxious expression, stood on the top step, peering inside. 'I'll go.'

He looked English—or American, perhaps. His face looked vaguely familiar. A typical teenager, growing rather too fast for his jeans, his beard a soft fuzziness on his chin, not yet shaveable. She unlocked the door. 'I'm sorry, but it is lunch time, you know. Who do you want to see?'

He was taller than Susanna. He looked down at her, with his anxiety fading, and a slow smile taking its place. He was carrying a canvas airline bag, but now he put it down, and held out his arms. 'Do I get a kiss, Susanna? I've come all the way from Sydney to see you.'

And of course she recognised him, and was delighted,

shocked and amazed, all at once. 'Matt! Matthew, my baby brother. What are you doing on this side of the globe? I thought you were doing A-levels in Harringay.' She hugged him hard, and their fair hair was exactly the same colour. For once, keeping her cap straight didn't matter. 'Oh, Matt, you were so small when I left. Just look at you—you're gigantic.'

'Only six two. I think I've stopped. Can I come in?'

She drew him happily inside, and locked the door again. 'Yes, of course. Come and meet Mei Li. How long are you staying? What happened to the A-levels?'

'I've finished the papers. I think I did all right, but I wasn't going to sit around at home waiting for the results. After all, when I do get into Medical School, I won't have two-month holidays any more. So I decided to see as much of the world as I could afford.'

'You'll stay with me?'

'Yes, please, I was counting on that. I'll earn my keep. I'm good at washing up.'

Mei Li was delighted for them. 'I can manage, Sue. Take the afternoon off.'

'I daren't. Not with Madam after my blood.'

Matt agreed. 'I want to look around a bit. If I could just leave my bag, I'll come back when you tell me.'

'Where do you want to go?'

'Thought I'd look for a job. I can stay longer then. I flew from Sydney with a couple of nice guys who're dossing around same as me, and I said I'd meet them later.' He gave a broad smile. 'What's on your mind, Sue? Think I'm going dope-smuggling or something?'

Susanna blushed. She *was* hoping Matthew hadn't got into bad company. 'People do it. All the time.'

'I wouldn't come straight to you, now, would I?'

'Possibly.' But his air was sincere and open and she smiled as she joked, 'I might be your cover.'

He snapped his fingers, as though he had forgotten something. 'Now, why didn't I think of that?' he teased.

As the two girls prepared for the afternoon session, they marvelled together at the adventurous spirit of today's youth—being themselves the grand ages of twenty-two and twenty. And Susanna's heart glowed with an excitement not even Tilly's account of their succulent oysters at the Goldleaf could dampen. And she hardly noticed that Dr Redfearn walked across the floor like a man in a trance, hardly acknowledging anyone.

Dr Carlton's diabetic patient was leaving the ward. His parents had come for him, and C.C. himself came down to speak to them, and see the boy off. Susanna left Mei Li in charge while she accompanied them to the front door, and stopped to chat to Dr Carlton for a while before he went back to work. 'Did you see Dr Redfearn's patient?'

'Yes, he discussed the case with me. The poor woman can't remember what happened before she came here. She doesn't know why she came, and she's no idea who she came to see. Beats me. Naturally, we don't know if she's epileptic, and ought to be on anticonvulsants all the time. He's leaving it till tomorrow to do an EEC —she seems too upset at not having any memory.'

'I suppose I could do no good if I went to see her?'

'It's worth a try, Susanna. After all, you are the only person here she spoke to before she came. Try to remember every word she said in that phone conversation, will you? Something she said might give us a clue.'

Susanna went across to the ward. She had to pass Gerry's door, and as she smiled at Amanda, she recalled the rather nice way Gerry had danced with her, the gentle compliments he paid, and the shivers that he evoked when he moved his strong fingers up and down her lumbar vertebrae. It had been really nice—but probably he meant nothing when he said they must have dinner sometime.

She had to cross a square of lawn to get to the residential side of the medical centre. It was laid out as a traditional Japanese garden, with lots of grey stone, a little brook that gurgled as it flowed downwards over green pebbles, and a small Buddhist shrine in miniature, with a curving roof, tiny tinkling bells to welcome the good luck spirits, and delicate gold carvings round the place where candles and incense could be burned. The sun was hidden, but the sky blazed with blue, and the palm leaves made fringed dark patterns against it. She sighed with pleasure. Life here was good. It had its ups and downs, but she did her best, and felt that it was appreciated. The Tillies of this world were always around, but they couldn't spoil her contentment at her life. And now that Matthew was here, it would be even nicer for a while.

She sat at Mrs Ming's bedside for about fifteen minutes. The poor woman was apprehensive, naturally. She kept murmuring 'Bridge, I know there was bridge.' But when Susanna asked her where, she only shook her head. Susanna stood up, and said gently, 'I'll come and see you again, dear.' As she moved away from the bed, the pathetic woman, in a borrowed nightdress, turned her head on the pillow, and closed her eyes in weariness.

Susanna could do no more. She walked along the corridor towards the door that led out to the Japanese garden. In one corner there was a wooden arbour, with a stone seat hidden under luxuriant creepers. She heard a noise, a rustle, and bent to look inside, in case a bird was trapped there. Instead, she opened her eyes in amazement and distress. Danny Redfearn sat there, leaning forward with his elbows on his knees. His smart tie was half pulled off, and in his hand was a wrinkled and torn photograph. His sweet, boyish face was tragic, bereft of all mischief now, the green eyes red-rimmed and old. And there were tears on his cheeks.

'Oh, I'm so sorry.' Her words were whispered in anguish at what she saw.

'It's all right, Valentine.' He tried to shake off his depression. 'It was daft of me to give way here. Sit with me for a while, lass, and tell me when I'll be fit to face society.'

'All right.' She sat by him, and her presence seemed to help. He turned and smiled. 'You look better now,' she said. But her own heart beat faster, at the shock of it all.

'Thank the good Lord it was you who found me.'

CHAPTER FOUR

ALTHOUGH that little episode had somehow made Susanna feel she knew Danny Redfearn rather better, he made no further reference to it. He always smiled at her, and was ready with a wink whenever they met, yet it was Tilly Paw he took out to lunch. And he didn't make any further attempt to chat for more than a few moments at a time. If Matthew had not been around, Susanna might have been puzzled. As it was she was busy and happy catching up on home news, and entertaining her lovely and very hungry baby brother. The Pagoda, from being the main part of her life, now assumed lesser proportions, as she dashed home each evening to 'mother' Matthew.

'It's like getting to know someone new,' she explained, when he laughingly asked what the inquisition was all about. 'You were a child when I left. Now you're a man, and a rather nice one too. I bet Mum and Dad are pretty proud of you.'

He didn't answer that one. 'Make the most of me while I'm here. If I get into Med. School, we won't have any more long holidays.'

'My brother a medical student!'

'Yes, medical students are really something else,' he teased. 'My theory is that they've got to be so darned respectable when they start work, that they make sure they sow lots of wild oats when they have the chance. One day—D.V.—I'll be a paragon of society—like that lot that you work with, Sue.' He reached in his pocket. 'I earned this in Chinatown this morning. Minded a chap's stall when his wife wanted him at home urgently.' He

50

produced three five-dollar bills. 'I'll pay for dinner.'

'You will not. But we'll eat out. I want you to see as much of my favourite city as you can.'

As they wandered in the neon-bright streets, enjoying the gentle warmth of the palm scented air, Susanna forgot her responsibilities as Administrator. She became just big sister again, chatting over old times, and window-gazing like any other tourist. 'Tell me about the boys you came with,' she asked.

'You'll probably meet them before long. We're all washing up at the Golden Dragon at eleven-thirty.' They were walking along a side street now, a pocket of quietness, where the traffic noise was muffled by floppy-leaved banana trees, and the lights were dimmer.

'Did you say they were English?'

'Bas is. He isn't a student. He's just dossing about because he likes it—and he's good at it too. Maybe his folks have money—I haven't asked. He's about sixteen, I guess. So's Jake, the Australian guy. They've both been to Singapore before.'

'Sixteen.' Susanna thought of herself as still a child at that age. 'I wonder if their parents worry.' She looked sharply at Matt. 'You've written regularly, I hope.'

'Don't worry. I send them a postcard from every city I visit.'

They wandered at random, admiring the skill of the Malay taxi-drivers, weaving round traffic jams with cowboy bravado. They passed groups of teenagers talking together. Secret societies? Smugglers? Somehow the exotic backcloth of the Singapore streets encouraged wild imagination. The kids were probably technical college students, talking over their day's lectures, and helping each other with the homework. Such was the magic of an oriental face, lending excitement to the common scene.

Her mind working overtime, Susanna asked, 'I

suppose you can look after yourself? Judo, that sort of thing?'

'Oh, sure. Bas had a bit of a shock in Sydney, when a couple of drunken yobs tried to beat him up—decided he was a Pommy bastard. Funny thing—the two words go together. All Pommies are bastards—and vice versa.'

'What happened?'

'Jake's ace at kung fu. I know a bit—enough to adopt a threatening pose, and make them think we were very dangerous. He's been training Bas and me. It gives you a lot of confidence, when you know how to defend yourself.'

'You're frightening me.'

'I'll get Jake to give you some lessons.'

They had reached the street markets in Lorong Chuan. 'This is the *pasar malam*,' explained Susanna. 'Every night they set up stalls in different places.'

'And where is the Thieves' Market? Bas said that was worth a visit.'

'That's in Sungei Road. But don't buy there, unless you are brilliant at bargaining.'

'I'm not bad—but I don't want to collect stuff anyway. Too heavy to carry.' He wandered among the stalls, with their gay streamers and coloured lanterns. 'They certainly know how to dress up.'

'The stalls are extra special this week, getting ready for National Day on August 9th.' She stopped by a small man whose stall consisted of a wooden tray balanced on his knees. And she bought a tiny gold charm, the Chinese letters for 'happiness'. 'There, that won't weigh you down, Matt.'

He threaded it on the chain he wore round his neck, with obvious delight. 'No young man yet, Sue?'

'That was a throwaway line, I must say. Mum asked you to find out, did she?'

'Not in so many words. But you're not bad looking,

you know. I thought you might be thinking of settling down.' And while her brother teased her, for some odd reason the green-eyed face of Danny Redfearn swam into her mind. 'Don't tell me no one's been smitten by your charms.'

'No. But I've been told that I'm going to turn into a bad-tempered old dragon.'

'Now that's significant. He must like you.' And Matt ducked, to evade Susanna's sudden poke in the ribs.

'You can tell them at home that I'm certain I made the right choice in coming here. And I love my job. They'll have to make do with that.' She had climbed on to a wooden fence, and sat like a schoolgirl, looking with sheer pleasure at the gaiety of the bustling streets, the tall apartment blocks lit up like Christmas trees, and beyond them the dark velvet sky studded with diamonds.

Next day was Thursday. Unexpectedly, Phil Chan needed Susanna in theatre for an emergency. 'Oh dear. Mei Li, would you mind doing the accounts? I haven't got them ready. I usually have them in rough before Friday.'

But Tilly was quick to show off her own efficiency. 'Don't, worry, Sue. I'll do it for you.' Her voice was just tinged with condescension. 'Perhaps it might be an idea to get a computer into here? It wouldn't take too long to train the existing staff.'

'Computer? For six doctors? I must dash. We'll discuss it later.' She didn't want a computer. She didn't want her system to be changed. She had this place running perfectly. That is, until Tilly Paw arrived, with her dainty prettiness, and her snake-like ability to poison the atmosphere.

'Thank you for coming.' Phil was, as usual, the perfect gentleman, always appreciative of what was done for him. 'And Danny wants the theatre next, to do an angiogram for Mrs Ming.'

'I've been to see her in the hospital. Poor lady, she's so unhappy about her memory.'

'Danny suspects a tumour in the durer. The CT scan showed a mass, almost certainly the cause of her forgetfulness. He wants to operate as soon as possible.'

While they were speaking, Jo-Jo was carefully administering the halothane to the comatose patient on the table. Susanna was not familiar with the operation Phil was doing, to open the front of the skull in order to remove a mass in the frontal sinus. But she was experienced enough at her job to be able to guess which instruments to lay out on her tray. And the initial stage consisted of slowly drilling holes in the bone, so that it could be neatly and safely removed, and later replaced. She watched, fascinated by the delicate skill in those hands, which were just as skilful with a golf club. As he drilled the precision holes, he chatted on as though they were just relaxing in the lounge. Except at the point where he had to lift the entire plate of bone away, when even Phil held his breath. Susanna swabbed, and murmured, 'Perfect.'

'Thank you, my dear. I always think that there is something of the actor in a surgeon. We do so love the applause.'

After that, the operation was not long. They were soon at the suture stage, and Phil was inserting a drainage tube. Susanna was relieved to see Redfearn had been watching the operation also, standing behind her where she did not see him. It would have unsettled her if she had known. Ever since she had seen him off-guard, revealing his vulnerability, she felt rather closer to him than she ought. Perhaps it was his quiet remark of appreciation—'Thank the good Lord it was you.' What did it mean? All she knew was that she was fond of all her doctors at the Pagoda, but this one was the only one to have a physical effect on her, a disturbing and unfamiliar effect.

Susanna went out to the changing room, pulling off her mask and gloves. She was quickly back in uniform, putting the last pin in her lace cap. There was a tap on the door. 'Yes?' She emerged into the corridor, to find Danny there. 'You are bringing Mrs Ming down now?'

'Yes, Valentine. If you aren't in a hurry, would you stay with her for a few moments, to calm her down. She seems fond of you.'

'Yes, of course. Do you want Dr Chou? He's in the recovery room with Phil's patient.'

'I know. I think I'll do this one under local.'

'Ugh. A bit painful.'

'You're right. But the operation isn't going to be easy, and I don't think it's too good for her to have two GAs in the space of a few days.'

'Do you mind me asking a question?'

'Fire away.'

'You are operating. Yet you don't call yourself "Mr" or put any surgical qualifications after your name.'

He gave a laconic grin. 'I thought it was easier to call myself Dr and be a neurologist. But I'm a fully qualified neurosurgeon as well. I just like a short name plate.'

'Yes, I thought you must be—it does give your FRCS in the book you wrote. Anyway, a neurologist wouldn't be writing about laser treatments, would he?'

'Well spotted, Valentine. Sheer modesty on my part. One of my few redeeming qualities.' He smiled at her, his eyes lingering on her face with that practiced charm she was getting used to. Then he looked up abruptly, as the trolley was brought down, with the pale form of Mrs Ming, her dark eyes misted with apprehension.

Susanna went at once to her. 'Don't be worried. You're in the very best possible hands.'

'Yes. Everyone says so.'

'And you still can't remember why you came to Dr Redfearn in the first place?'

'No. I'd swear I'd never heard of him. But I must have, mustn't I?'

'You have. Because when you phoned, you asked specifically for him.'

The woman sighed, the white sheet over her thin body rising and falling as she did. 'Oh, well, I'm glad he's clever.' She reached for Susanna's hand. 'You have been so very kind.'

'I'll come and see you when this is all over,' Susanna promised. She paused at the theatre entrance, where Danny was chatting to Jo-Jo. 'Would you let me know the results?'

Danny smiled. 'Yes, Valentine. I'll come and tell you myself.'

'Thank you. I've calmed her a little, I think.'

'Bless you.'

Back at her desk, Susanna found that the week's figures were perfectly written down and added up. More of Tilly's efficiency. Why was she irritated by it, when she ought to be relieved they were all done? And Phil's jokey words came back to her. 'Of course women can be the best of friends—so long as there isn't a man in the case.' A man . . . and she blushed a little, recognising jealousy in herself, and not liking it much. Thank goodness she had Matthew to go home to. He would cheer her up, and take her mind off Tilly Paw.

'Oh, Susanna?'

A musical and delicate voice, an unmistakable voice. 'Yes, Tilly?'

'You have written on Mrs Ming's notes that she's had this angiogram, as well as a Cat scan and an ECG?'

'Dr Redfearn has. Why? It's usual.'

'I didn't want anyone to forget. They all cost money, you know.'

'Money!' Susanna tried not to retort. How could she think of money, when the sight of that white, tense little face over the white sheet was all that Susanna thought about?

'Well, it did occur to me that she's getting all this expensive treatment, and she might have no money at all. She might not even have come to see Danny professionally. She might have come to ask for a job, or something.' Tilly clearly thought she was a sharp little businesswoman, to have thought of that.

Another voice joined in the conversation. Danny had come across without being noticed by the girls. His naturally pleasant voice sounded hard, suddenly. 'Miss Paw, when someone is seriously ill, a doctor only thinks of what he can do to help. He doesn't demand a look at her bank statement.' His voice rose in anger.

She matched him, tone for tone. 'Then he ought to, Dr Redfearn. This isn't a charity hospital. There are enough of them in this city. She could easily have been transferred. We are in business to make money, not to treat beggars.'

Susanna stood, unable to walk away from this exchange. She watched them facing each other, each face handsome but determined. His voice was very low now. 'Then, to set your mind at rest, I'll pay for the damn tests myself. And operate for nothing.'

Susanna watched Tilly's face. Surely that would make her ashamed. But she only said coolly, 'And what about the hospital charges?'

Susanna couldn't stand aside any longer. 'I'll pay them, Tilly. And I'd better make a note of that now, so that no one is in any doubt about who is paying what.'

But the icy words had no effect. Tilly either didn't understand the sarcasm, or decided to ignore it. She

said, 'Yes, please. We'd be out of business, Danny, if
we all thought like you. The job of an administrator,
Susanna, is to manage a business, not to dole out
charity.'

'I'm quite aware what my job is.' Susanna wanted to
argue. She wanted to point out that the Pagoda was
doing excellent business, and that one single act of
kindness would bankrupt no one. But there seemed no
chance of her words getting through, so she turned away
towards the office.

To her intense surprise, Tilly put on a little-girl voice
almost at once. 'I'm lunching at the Colony, Danny.
Coming?'

Susanna hastened her steps, and closed the office
door. She didn't want to hear whether Danny accepted
the invitation or not. But the murmur of voices went on
for a while, showing that he had not rejected her with the
scorn she deserved.

When she opened the door again, there was no one in
the foyer. Oh well, she didn't care who lunched with
who, did she? Gerry Sovani appeared, escorting his
last morning patient to the door. 'That should give no
more trouble, Mrs Jinnah.' The same familiar phrases
sounded so smooth and delightful when said by Gerry in
his gentle, faintly-accented English. 'Please do not eat
on that side for a couple of hours, will you for me? No,
no further treatment is necessary. Yes, my receptionist
will be happy to send for you again in three months.
Good morning, Mrs Jinnah.'

Yes, that must be another matron, enamoured of her
dentist. It was obvious by the ratio of females to males
that Gerry did more business on his sex-appeal than his
skill, both of which were considerable. Oh well, if it
made them happy, they got excellent dentistry as well as
the thrill of his dark eyes, the closeness of his smooth
brown face. Susanna went back to her desk. But in

seconds, Gerry had despatched Mrs Jinnah down the steps, and had crossed the floor in a couple of long strides. 'Susanna.'

'Hello, Gerry. Off for lunch? Shall I put your white coat back?'

'What? Oh, yes.' He pulled it off while he was talking. 'I was wondering if you were free at all this weekend?'

This was it, then. She was really receiving an invitation from the heart-throb of Gold Hill Plaza. But she wasn't free. 'I'm afraid my brother is staying with me. He's only got a few weeks before he has to go back to start Medical School in Edinburgh.'

'How nice for you. He didn't fancy Dentistry, then? No, few boys do. Yet it is a steady job, with a minimum of physical strain, and the remuneration is good and the hours delightful. Jo-Jo accuses me of drilling for gold —and he isn't very wrong.'

'You don't do it for the money, I'm sure.' She teased him a little.

'No, certainly not. I was joking—I think.' He patted her hand as she took his coat from him. 'I'm off for lunch. See you later.' And he ran lightly down the steps, saying no more about the weekend. Oh well, perhaps another time . . .

Mei Li came bustling in. 'I'm starving. Hi, Sue, how's Mrs Ming?'

'Still in theatre.'

'How did Phil's operation go?'

'Tremendously. He's a genius.'

Mei Li grinned. 'I wish some of his genius would rub off on me. I can never think of anything clever to say to Tilly. She's always scoring points against me. I can only think of clever things when I'm by myself.'

'I wouldn't want to be clever in her way.' Susanna related the story of Tilly's insistence that Mrs Ming's bills be met. 'Now I don't think that is human. Maybe that's why she wants a computer. She wants someone to talk to that speaks her language.'

Mei Li laughed, but then she sighed. 'She's so very pretty.'

'Handsome is as handsome does. You are miles prettier than she is.'

'She dresses so well. And makes it look easy.'

'It is easy when you're a millionairess.'

'And she always knows exactly what to say to a man. I wish I could have that one gift.'

Susanna smiled. 'I can't argue with that. I'm afraid I'm as green with envy as you. Are we cowards, do you think, or is it that if you have a lot of money it just gives you more confidence in everything?'

'It never bothered us before. We were so happy here before she came. Now she's upsetting just about everyone.' Mei Li sighed again. Then she brightened. 'Never mind. I've just bought some of Mr Lim's prawn crackers. I don't know what he puts in them, but they're miles better than anyone else's. Have some.'

'Thank you. You see, you always have your priorities right.' And they sat at their ease, munching crackers, and drinking green tea.

'Valentine?'

They sat up, startled, although there was no secret about who it was, marching into the office with athletic strides. Susanna stood up, wiping her fingers on a tissue. 'How is she?'

'Okay. The blood vessels are clear enough. The question is, how many will I have to tie off altogether.'

Mei Li said meekly, 'Would you like a prawn cracker?'

He sat down, and stretched his legs before him. 'I'd love one.' He turned to Susanna. 'Did you mean that about paying Mrs Ming's charges?'

'Yes, of course I did. I've written it down now.'

'And I'll help.' Mei Li handed the crackers, and Danny took a handful.

'Thanks. I feel so desperately sorry for the poor creature. There is absolutely nothing in her handbag, apart from a few dollars and a handkerchief. It is obviously the effects of the tumour. She must have been like this for a while, so my guess is that she lives alone.'

'I'll start phoning all the Mings in the book, shall I?' Susanna stood up, ready to begin at once.

'Hey, have your break first. It's not that vital. Yet—' he shrugged, 'I can't help thinking over what Tilly said—about her coming to see me for quite a different reason, not a medical one at all.'

'And have you any idea what it might be?'

He looked down, and Susanna stood watching his bowed head, feeling terribly sad, without knowing why. His fingers were twisting together, but he quickly pulled himself together and sat up straight, realising the girls were watching him. Then he said slowly, 'It's this bridge she was talking about.'

'You know which one she meant?'

'It might have been a name—Bridget. That's the name of my late wife. She'd left me years ago, and she took our son. That's why I came out here. To try and find out what happened to them.'

Susanna and Mei Li stared, unable to think of anything comforting to say. Susanna said hesitantly, 'Didn't she write to you?'

'No.' He smiled. 'I might be barking up the wrong tree. My lawyers couldn't find any trace of them—not surprising, as she changed her name of course, when she came out here.' He stood up. 'Never mind. I'll operate. If she recovers her memory, things will sort themselves out.'

'And she will recover it?'

'Most likely. The worry is that those blood vessels are

vital ones, and the operation will leave her paralysed on one side. That's why I'd be so glad to know she had someone to care for her afterwards.' He was still on his feet, but somehow seemed reluctant to go. It had helped him, being able to mention a little of his problem to them. 'Funny sort of life, isn't it? So much hurt in the world, yet so much brilliance, so much money. Have you even been hurt, Valentine?'

'No.' It seemed wrong to say that, to this man whose raw agony was patent in the quiet room. 'I've got this policy of planning life so that I don't put myself in danger of being hurt.'

He seemed to forget his own problems for a moment. He said in a low, urgent voice, 'Oh, Valentine, you mustn't do that. It's better to be hurt than not to live.'

'But I am living.'

'Are you?' He looked across at Mei Li. 'Are you living, Mei Li?'

'Maybe not yet. But I'm only twenty.'

'True. You're both young. But don't be afraid of life. Don't ever fear it. It's mighty and unpredictable—and yes, you do get hurt. But it's a glorious experience for all that—a challenge, Valentine. Treat it as a challenge.'

Susanna turned away, and pretended to straighten her cap at the mirror, though it was already perfectly straight. Her fingers trembled, and she didn't know why. 'Even if your wife leaves you?'

'Oh, well, it was a long time ago. Ten years, more. She said I neglected her for my work. Maybe I did, but I didn't think so. Work was hard as a junior in my time. I sure as dammit tried to please her.' He took one more step towards the door, then turned back. He wanted to speak.

Susanna knew what he wanted to say. 'We won't tell a soul. But I'll keep at the phone book, in the hope that we'll find a relative for you.'

'For her sake just as much as mine.' He left them then, and they were both too overwhelmed by the emotion in the air to want to say anything for a while.

Then Susanna spoke. 'The fool. The stupid, selfish fool.'

'Hey, steady on. I like him.'

'Not Danny—Bridget. How could she leave such a man? When he was working at his career? She should have supported him all along the way.'

'I don't expect he's the first man to marry the wrong woman.'

'No.' Susanna tried to suppress her fury at this unknown woman. 'I'm glad he told me. I'll be able to question Mrs Ming in more detail. She might have known Bridget. Maybe that's why she came.'

'I don't think you should raise his hopes, Sue. The woman has a brain tumour. She came to see a neurologist. It would be a very great co-incidence if she knew his wife as well, wouldn't it? I think he's clutching at straws.'

Susanna sat down, remembering the tears on his face, the photograph he clutched. All she wanted was to be able to help him. She walked home a long way round. She wanted time to think, to absorb what Danny had told her. It seemed so perfectly natural to want to help him. Yet, apart from paying her some very genuine compliments—and she did think they were genuine—he had not gone out of his way to influence her at all. His behaviour had been quite proper, quite detached. So she decided it must be her own decision, to want to give him some sort of support and help—to try, in fact, to take away that terrible sadness from his eyes.

His marital problems were nothing to do with her. She found her thoughts were being drowned by Chinese music from one of the night markets in the next street. She wandered around to the stalls, pleasing her eyes by the colourful lanterns, the painted dragons and lions festooned with gold and silver tinsel. The sheer profusion delighted her. And as she paused to breathe in the heavy smell of incense in the air, she recalled Danny's advice. *Live! Don't be afraid to live. All life is a challenge.* And she recognised in herself the hunger for life, that so far she had so neatly and carefully refused to acknowledge.

She retraced her steps, understanding herself more. The attraction to Danny Redfearn was because she saw in him a similar spirit to her own. There need be nothing more than that in their relationship. Calmer in mind, she stopped and idly fingered the silken good-luck charms, dangling provocatively from a painted stick, inviting her to buy. The tassels felt soft and gentle to her fingers. The smoke from the joss sticks was almost too sickly sweet. She picked up a scarlet spell, written in gold, and the stall holder was quick to tell her that with that she would dispel all the bad spirits that sought to harm her.

Susanna smiled at him, and tinkled one of the many lucky silver bells that also hung from the stall, catching the breezes in the warmth of the night. Then she replaced the charm. 'Tomorrow, maybe,' she said, and turned for home.

CHAPTER FIVE

THE sun edged behind the Gold Hill tower. Time to check the figures for Mrs Paw's Friday phone call. Susanna methodically went down the list, double-checking what she already knew had been thoroughly checked by the redoubtable Tilly. She carried out the work almost automatically, because she was still thinking of Danny. She hadn't seen him come in today, and somehow she wanted to see if he had regained his cheerful twinkle. Even though last night she had rationalised her feelings, she found she still could not get out of her mind that dull ache of sympathy with him.

She had spent much of the day telephoning all the Mings in the book, with no success. She had pencilled in the numbers where there had been no reply, so that they could be tried again. Poor Mrs Ming, the lady without even a first name, lying so still and unhappy wondering who she was.

The phone rang. 'Pagoda Medical Centre?'

It was Mrs Paw. 'Hello, Susanna. Could I have a word with Tilly, dear? Is she there?'

'Not here, Mrs Paw. I'll find her and ring you back.'

'Good girl.' Patronising of course. Susanna knew that Mrs Paw got very irritated if she was made to hold on. She said her time was money, and one paid people to hold on for one. But Susanna was hurt. Mrs Paw was ringing for the week's figures, and she had asked for Tilly, not Susanna herself. Then she shrugged her shoulders and started buzzing the various suites. She had been in Singapore long enough to know that people who cared

65

about money didn't necessarily dislike the human race, it was just a question of understanding their priorities. If Ellen Paw wanted the figures from Tilly instead of Susanna, then that was her own affair.

'Hello? Is Tilly there, please?'

She finally reached her in Suite Six, and felt again a buzz of jealousy. What was Tilly doing up there? Danny wasn't busy. He'd only had four patients all week—naturally enough, as his name wasn't even on the plate outside yet. She was waiting for it to be put up this afternoon. 'Yes, Susanna? Who wants me?'

'Your mother.' Susanna couldn't help one small dig at Tilly. 'By the way, Danny isn't busy. Shouldn't you be assisting in some other office?'

'He has no patients, but he's explaining what tests he has to do. It is most interesting.' And she said it in such a sweet voice, that Susanna wished she hadn't said anything. Tilly knew she was jealous. What a humiliating situation. From now on, she would keep quiet. It was hard not to think of them up there, Tilly casually sitting on the desk looking like some oriental goddess, and Danny leaning back, smiling up at her with that wonderful, narrow-eyed smile . . .

Within minutes, Tilly herself was stepping lightly out of the lift. Susanna looked down to hide the tinge of colour in her cheeks. 'I'll take it here if you don't mind, Sue. Mummy will be calling about the figures. Do you mind?' And she waited while Susanna vacated her chair, then took her place, and spread out the finished accounts in front of her. 'Would you get the number, please?' So sweet, so courteous. Susanna fumed, and pressed the buttons that Tilly could easily have done herself.

'Hello? Tilly Paw to speak to Mrs Paw.'

'Mummy?' She slipped into Chinese for a moment. Susanna turned away. 'Yes, it's great here, really interesting. I thought may be a computer in the office

—and a word processor? You know, that agent we met at the Trade Fair . . . Shanghai? What about Paris? Oh, I see. Yes, I'll talk it over with you. Tonight? I'm busy for dinner—no, I couldn't possibly . . . Don't be silly, dear. We're good friends—and he's marvellous company . . . All right. See you later.'

Marvellous company. Susanna left Tilly making further phone calls, and made her way out to the back of the building. Let her get her own numbers. There was little doubt who she was having dinner with. Susanna went out into the Japanese garden and sat down on a low stone wall, gazing into the rippling stream.

There was no harm in them dining together. He was a nice chap, lonely, probably. Tilly would be entertaining company. But again Susanna felt a sense of loss. She was outside Tilly's bright successful world. Yet until Tilly Paw had arrived here, Susanna had thought her life was totally delightful and fulfilled. Was it Tilly, or was it Danny Redfearn who had turned her world upside down?

It was a double loss. Danny didn't belong to her, so she couldn't really claim Tilly had stolen him. Yet she had muscled in on Danny. And today it was quite clear that she had muscled in on Susanna's job as well. She was making the decisions about computers and word processors. She was doing the accounts, and telling 'Mummy' how much she loved the place. She pulled at some grasses, dropping them slowly into the tiny stream. She was totally unwanted here. Although it was afternoon, she felt a cloud of gloom enfolding her in the warm, decorative garden. She could fight another woman for her job—but not the Boss's daughter. That wasn't a fair fight. She had no chance at all.

'Hey Valentine. Happy anniversary. What are you doing out in the midday sun?'

She looked up. He stood against the white walls, his

slim figure erect—and so welcome—with the dark
spikes of greenery making a vivid backcloth against the
blue sky. She smiled with a surge of pleasure. 'It isn't
midday. It's nearly five o'clock.'

'I know that. That's why I came. It's exactly a week
since we met.' He crossed the crazy paved path towards
her—and in seconds the drabness had vanished from
the little garden and it was bright, cheerful and perfect,
with the addition of one affectionate and sympathetic
human being.

She looked up at him, glad to see that his face was
calm, and his eyes no longer showing traces of sadness.
No sign of his secret today, and she would not mention it
either. She was just so wonderfully glad to see him. She
was able to joke. 'You remembered!'

'I did indeed. But last week you were madly busy.
What are you doing idling away like my flaxen-haired
girl?'

'You know what I'm doing. You passed my desk. You
saw . . .' she stopped. No, she would not be vindictive.
She took a deep breath, and tossed the last sliver of grass
into the water. 'I'm delegating. The first rule of any
General,' she said lightly.

He nodded. He knew very well what was going on.
And to his credit he did not pursue the subject. 'Some
General.' His appreciative words sounded like some soft
breeze from his gentle native hills.

Susanna bit her lip, and looked down hard at the
water, catching the sunlight reflected off the white walls.
The very worst thing when you are feeling sorry for
yourself is for someone to be sympathetic.

Especially when he was standing so very close, and
was so sweet, so kind—and so attractive. It was impossible not to feel it. She could feel his warmth, smell his
sweat—a strangely personal link. Beads formed on his
sunburnt forehead where that waving lock of hair kept

falling, only to be swept away with the back of his capable, surgeon's hand.

She had to be practical, or she would have wept. 'How is Mrs Ming?'

'Calm. She's looking forward to the operation now, bless her, to get the thing over and remember something. The angiograms weren't quite as hopeless as I thought at first. I think the main cerebral artery will be intact. I just hope she has someone to look after her. I daren't keep her in hospital too long, in view of Madame Money's attitude.' Madame Money? He couldn't be all that smitten then, could he?

'I suppose we might ask the police to broadcast an SOS?'

'That might work, Valentine.'

'If it doesn't, then I've decided what to do. She's fond of me I think. She can stay at my flat. My maid doesn't mind coming in every day. It isn't far away, and she won't be getting bills from me.'

He didn't answer right away, but she knew he was looking down at her, and she daren't meet his look. 'Thanks, Valentine.'

'And anyway, I still have some numbers to try in the phone book.'

'You've done enough. Give me the list and I'll have a go.'

'No, don't worry. I've got the time. And you're going out.' She bit her lip. She shouldn't have said that. It was none of her business.

'Hey Valentine, does it matter? That much?' His voice was a bit puzzled now.

With studied calm, she said, 'Of course not. And thank you for coming down to remind me of our anniversary.' Then daring to meet his gaze, she managed a smile. 'You've certainly livened the place up in one short week.'

'And I want to apologise to you. I called you a dragon spider. You are nothing of the kind, Valentine, so will you forgive me, and say we're friends?'

'I daresay I will. But you've only known me a week. I could be all sorts of spider and you don't realise.'

His voice was relaxed now. She was glad she had managed to show him how little he meant to her. He said, 'When I've done what I came to do, Spider, I'd like to know you better. I am forgiven, then, am I?'

'You know you are. You always get your own way I'm sure. Being a leprechaun? One of the little people?' She had a smile in her eyes, facing him now, feeling totally at ease with him. It was a feeling she wanted to hold on to, but knew she couldn't for long.

'What?' Laughing, he attempted to catch her, but she evaded his hand, and crossed the tiny bridge, so that the stream was between them. She knew she didn't want him too close. Because if they spoke any deeper, any deeper than their happy words and laughter, they would find the deepest parts, where the tenderness was, where there could be so much hurt.

They faced each other. He said, keeping his face straight, 'You ought to get back to your desk, Sister Valentine. You might be needed.'

'You're right.' He had cheered her up, and she decided that it was safe to return over the bridge. But the moment she was on his side of the stream, he caught her arm, and swung her to face him, his six feet towering over her five. 'One of the little people, am I? Well, Valentine, you may or may not be a spider, but you certainly need an urgent Eye Test.' It was only a joke. They were only playing, in that small enchanted square of garden. But the impetus of his pull had brought her into the circle of his arms, and he did not take them away, but clasped his hands together around her. She was trapped by his lean brown arms, close against the full length of his body. It was a sweet place to be, and there was a bubble of brightness in her heart at that moment that she dare not move to burst. It was only a moment in a little horseplay, but it was exquisite.

Then she began to panic. He was in no hurry to break their magic ring. Perhaps she was frightened because the green eyes had a look that she had not seen before, and she knew she was helpless to break the embrace. She had abdicated her own will to the whim of this impertinent, impossible, unique man. He looked at her, his eyes moving as he took in the full shape of her face. 'Isn't it time you let me go, Valentine?' he whispered. 'I have work to do, witch.'

'If you hadn't already noticed, it is you holding me.'

'Is it?' And the grip tightened a little more. Susanna did not object in the slightest. 'Oh, but it's your fault.'

She was able to do something then, because she knew that at the same time as he was weaving this tangle of ephemera about her, Tilly Paw was waiting in the foyer to take him off to dinner—and he was not going to decline. She was a momentary diversion in his afternoon. And it riled her because it was so much more to her. Tilly Paw was waiting on the sidelines to take over not only her job, but her man, the first one she had ever felt about in this exhilarating, terrifying way. 'I have to go now.'

He felt her yielding body stiffen, and allowed his hands to fall to his sides. 'There's never enough time. So you have to go.' Even his gentle voice was torture to her now, such were her feelings tautened by his presence. 'Meet me here in a year's time, Valentine.'

'You think we'll both be here?'

'Who knows? Only the wind.' He paused. She heard then the chirping of the grasshoppers and the chirruping of the Indian sparrows in the tall palms above them. 'But it would be nice to think so. Wouldn't it?'

She felt a constriction in her throat, stopping her speech. She felt that if the situation was the same, with a Tilly Paw gloating over her, she could stand no more than today. Trying not to run, she turned away .and walked back inside, with the imprint of his windswept hair round his tanned, explorer's face, the stance of his vital body, legs apart as though bracing himself against the world, lingering across her eyes, misting what was really there.

Tilly had vanished. Slowly Susanna's eyes got used to indoors, and she went into the office to complete the usual Friday affairs. She sat down at Mei Li's desk, taking several deep breaths of air that she was not sharing with Danny Redfearn, and a large tear blobbed suddenly on the pile of mail before her. Hastily she dabbed at it with her handkerchief, and smeared at her eyes, before anyone noticed.

'All right, Sue?'

'Yes, of course!'

'Only asked.'

'Sorry, Mei Li.'

'You've been talking to Danny, haven't you? He came and asked where you were, and Tilly said she didn't know, but I told him.'

Susanna didn't reply, pretending to be very busy with the papers on the desk. Mei Li said softly, 'It's all right, you know. He's the original charmer. You're not the only one. The entire female staff have fallen for him. He doesn't mean any harm. He's just—well, he just has this power. Ask Amanda, ask Rayah. He makes every girl feel special when he looks at her in that certain way. Just admit it, then it won't feel so bad.'

'Why won't it?' Susanna was jerked out of her self-pity by Mei Li's worldly-wise kindness. 'And why do you know more about it than I do? I'm two years older than you.'

'Well,' Mei Li twirled the stool she was sitting on to face Susanna. 'He's a nice guy, right? So he isn't turning on the charm to get any of us into bed, is he? He came here to do a job—and he admitted to us that he hoped he might turn up some trace of his family while he was here. But if you think he wants to get entangled with anyone else while he's here, I'd say it would be the last thing he'd want.'

'That sounds very sensible to me.'

'So, instead of weeping in the corner, admit that you've been charmed as well. It'll pass off. I used to dream about James Bond. I couldn't stop thinking about him.' She smiled, her lively, infectious smile. 'But I survived, didn't I?'

'All right, Auntie, so how do you rate Little Tilly? He seems to have allowed her to get past the "just good friends" stage in one easy lesson.'

'To be completely honest, Sue, my opinion of that lady is probably the same as yours—she is what they call one tough cookie, right?'

'Absolutely right.'

'If a man didn't want to get involved—isn't that the sort he'd go out with, just to pass the long lonely nights? One that won't get hurt? One he doesn't have to be sincere with?'

Susanna allowed herself to relax. 'Mei Li, you are amazing. But I think you're probably on the right track. Thanks.' She turned back to the desk, knowing she ought to be comforted. But as she lifted the account sheets, one by one, to return to each individual doctor's file, she felt such overwhelming, ravening waves flowing around her ears as though she were literally drowning. She had to stop for a while, and bend her head as though to revive herself after a faint. This was just a crush? Mei Li might be right; all she knew was that these feelings were terribly real, and wouldn't go away. She saw him, heard him as she methodically went back to work. She felt him dominating her entire brain. She went over and over those sweet warm words he had said to her this afternoon. Yet there must have been part of her thinking apparatus still unscathed, because she finished the filing in good time and made not a single mistake. Perhaps it was because all she wanted was to hurry home and bury her face in a cushion.

'Oh Susanna. You are going home early?'

'Hello Gerry.' She had already changed into her blue cotton dress, and her high-heeled sandals, and collected her white kid bag. She was feeling calmer now, thankful that the human body was able to recover from such emotional onslaughts as she had felt that afternoon. She smiled up at him, her own immaculate dentist, and there was approval in his dark-eyed response.

'You are in a hurry to get back to your brother?'

'Not really.' It was refreshing to talk to Gerry. His hair was so splendidly perfect, his tie so elegantly tied, and his shoes so beautifully shiny. Not much of the explorer type here—thank goodness. No hassle. No breathless distraction. Gerry was neat, predictable, and so very comfortingly un-overwhelming. Yet it was an honour to be seen with him, so popular was he with Singapore's smart set. She waved a hand casually, and repeated the lines she had learned that afternoon. 'I'm learning to delegate. I'm making good use of Tilly and Mei Li.'

'You are very wise.' He put out an elegant hand as she showed signs of going. 'Susanna, I was wondering— there is a small party on Sunday night. The Mettiar family has invited a few friends. I would like to take you and your brother—that is, of course, if he likes Indian food.'

'The Mettiars—your most faithful patients.'

'And friends.' They would be. One of the richest families.

'And you're sure—Matthew and I—'

'They asked me most particularly to bring someone from the Pagoda.'

'What about Amanda?'

'She cannot. She goes home to Malacca every weekend.'

Susanna reflected that Matt would enjoy a typically Indian meal—especially in the sumptuous surroundings of the Mettiars. And she herself would be much happier to be in the comparatively calm and unemotional environment of the polite and gentle Mettiars. 'If Matthew has made no other arrangements, we'd be very happy to accept.'

'Wonderful. I'll call you before then, to arrange where to meet.'

She watched him precede her down the steps. He waved before merging into the crowds of home-bound commuters. Night was almost upon them, the turquoise of the sky already pierced with points of brilliants. The joss sticks from the temple close by were not yet strong enough to penetrate the warm smell of hot curry and satay at the street stalls.

Gerry was a man on her wavelength—wasn't he? They were both very methodical, neat, and stylish in their dress. He was classically handsome, and his regular features and deep liquid eyes could please the eyes without brutally assaulting the senses as someone else's narrow green gaze was capable of doing. She had known Gerry over four years. Each time she saw him out, it was with a different gorgeous woman. His taste was good. They were all pretty, with shining hair, and good legs . . . She ought to be highly flattered, to be finally chosen as his latest escort. And he had shown how kind he was by inviting Matthew too. That was the final touch. It would be a privilege.

'Hi, Sue. The lads are here.'

She entered into a room—was this her room? Records and tapes were scattered all over the floor, plus several newspapers and seven coffee mugs. Matt lay on the sofa, looking through some sheet music. One other boy, with carrotty hair and freckles, sat on the arm of a chair, eating a hamburger. And the third, rather quieter and darker haired, set crosslegged on the floor amid the mess, strumming at an ancient acoustic guitar. She smiled. 'I see the lads are here. Hello. Nice to meet you.'

The dark-haired one said in slightly American English, 'Hi, Sue. Matt said you wouldn't mind.' He put the guitar on one side, and pulled himself up. He was lithe and thin, and very untidy. But his eyes were sharp, and his smile genuine. 'I'm Bas.'

'How do you do. And you're Jake?'

'Yeah.' Jake's smile was slightly less trusting. But he was neater, which made up for a lot. 'Hope you don't mind the smell of hamburgers.'

'Of course I don't.' She stepped lightly over the debris. 'I can see you don't want any more coffee. But is there anything else I can get you.'

'No thanks. I've got a gig in town. If you've finished with the instrument, Bas, I'll be on my way.'

Matthew said, 'What time you have to be there?'

'Gig doesn't start till eleven.' He smiled again, wrinkling his freckly nose. 'Until then, I'm a waiter. See you.'

'You mean you're a waiter and washer-up, and you're going to play the guitar if they don't stop you,' called Matthew just before the door slammed behind his friend. He looked apologetically at Susanna. 'I'll tidy up.'

'Don't worry now. Let's go out. I'll treat you both.'

Bas said, 'I didn't know sisters were like that. I thought they always made a fuss.' And Susanna forgave him at once for his untidy appearance. And she liked him even more, when she came back from having a shower and changing. The boys had washed the mugs, and straightened the room. It wasn't quite its usual pristine elegance, but it was a good try for teenagers, and Susanna expressed her delight at once.

'Where would you like to eat?'

Bas said, 'There's a place in Changi. Is it too far to go?'

'Of course not. We've got all night. What place is this, Bas?'

'Somewhere I used to go when I lived there.'

'I see.' She didn't want to pry. He gave an impression of a young wild animal, friendly but cautious. A wrong move, even a wrong word, and Bas would fade into the undergrowth. 'Am I all right in these trousers?' She was wearing cool cotton pants, and a loose fitting blue blouse with a round, lowish neck that showed off her tan.

'Great.'

'I'll just do my hair.'

'Don't, Sue.' Matthew was waiting at the door. 'It looks better like that.'

'Down? Honestly?'

Bas interrupted again. 'Down. Perfect, honest.'

She smiled at him. 'You have lots of self confidence.'

'I learned to have.' He grinned suddenly. 'Better make a start. There's a bus for Changi in ten minutes. I'll tell you my life story some other time.'

Susanna followed them out and locked the door. Privately she felt that Bas had hardly lived long enough to write his life story—but then it was obvious that he had seen more of life than he perhaps would have chosen. She wondered if it was prying to ask. 'You chose it, Bas?'

As they settled themselves on the bus, he didn't seem to mind talking. 'I chose it, sure. I had a few dollars in the bank, so I decided to see the world when my mum died. Not like Matthew here, O-levels and A-levels and University.'

'Well, it's a living. I've always wanted to be a doctor, even when I was little. I don't know if it was because our GP had a shiny silver Aston Martin, though. I'll let you know that one.' Susanna felt a pride in her brother. He didn't try and be a conformist. He stood up for what he believed in.

'I daresay I'll settle down some time. My dad was a doctor.'

Something rang in Susanna's mind. Be careful, careful . . . 'Where was this?'

'Somewhere remote. Outskirts of Southampton, I think. I don't remember him. He left us, anyway. He didn't want us, so we didn't want him.' Bas had a nice, rather shy way of talking, that took away the harshness of his words. Susanna felt her heart begin to race.

'Do you know any of the doctors at the Pagoda, Bas?'

'No idea. I've been in Sydney for a year. Before that it was California.' He looked out of the window. 'You know, it's good to be back. I only came because the lads persuaded me to when we were dossing in Sydney harbour. But I'm glad I came. It's the place I've lived in the longest.'

He went on to tell them some of his adventures. 'Washing up's the easiest way to get cash, but someone I met in California gave me that old guitar. That was great. A couple of chords, and a verse or two of "Yellow Submarine" or "Shenendoah" and I always had the price of a doss if I needed it. But I got to like sleeping outside.'

'All right if there are no mosquitoes.'

They had passed the time quickly. 'Here we are.' Bas stood up and ran for the door, as the bus was almost starting off. The others followed him, and they jumped off, laughing. Then Bas started running out of sheer animal spirits, and Susanna and Matt ran too. Her hair

flowed out behind her as she ran, feeling suddenly as
happy and carefree as she had when a child. It must
be the loose hair—or the soft-soled sandals. When
Matthew was a baby, and she had been allowed to push
him if she didn't run, in his little push chair.

They were running up a steepish narrow street, with
terraces of Chinese houses, with their slatted shutters,
and their mirrors over the door, and their good-luck
charms and National Day decorations looped from the
tiny balconies. The lighting was dim, not like the centre
of Changi. Suddenly Bas disappeared. 'Where did he
go?'

Matt pointed. 'Down those steps.' Stone steps led to a
basement, where the light was much brighter, and a fan
gave blessed cool breezes to the three of them after their
short run. Several small tables were occupied by Chinese
families. Theirs were the only white faces.

Bas had sat down in a corner. There was a smart red
and white tablecloth and a tiny Chinese brass pot con-
taining a single hibiscus blossom. There was a look on his
modest face that was of real pleasure, almost emotion.
He beckoned them over—to stares from the rest of the
clientele. But Bas took no notice. And as the others sat
down, he pulled unceremoniously at the apron strings of
a chubby Chinese waiter who had his back to them.
'Hey, how about some service here, Say Lun?'

The man turned, ready with an angry retort. But at the
sight of the boy, he opened his great arms, dropping his
notebook on the floor, and poured out a string of
Chinese, as he embraced him. 'Where you been, son?'

'Out and around, Say Lun. Australia, California, you
name it, I've seen it. Say Lun, where's Ma? I've got a
couple of special friends here. Sue and Matt. From
London, man. You're not impressed?'

The man opened his arms to them, as though to
embrace them all. 'Hey, nice to see you.' He called, 'Ma,

come here, lah. Here's Bas and two friends.'

A thin grey-haired woman came from the back, limping a little. Her small wizened face lit up, the dark eyes gleaming with joy. 'Oh Bas, we do miss you for so long, lah.'

The boy went over to give her a firm hug and an unembarrassed kiss. 'You're limping, Ma. Rheumatism bad again?'

'Only since you go, lah. Better you come back, stay with us now.' She looked at him, smiling, her face transformed with its emotion. It might have been her own son she was looking at. She pushed some stray wisps of hair back, and took the stained little menu away from the table. 'Now you sit right there. Ma bring you best meal you ever had. And then you stay, Bas?'

'Your cooking always could work miracles, Ma.'

She murmured something in Cantonese. What she said didn't matter. It was obvious that here was a home, if ever Bas wanted one. And it was significant that it was almost the first place he had wanted to come back to. Up till tonight, he was talking only of moving on, as Matthew went on to say, 'You like it here, Bas. Why don't you stay, and do A-levels? Who knows, we might both end up as Pagoda doctors? How does that grab you?'

'Don't tie me down, man.'

Susanna took his side. 'Yes, Matt, don't bully the boy. He's been a citizen of the world long enough to make his own decisions.'

The boy looked across at her, and she met his look, vainly searching for some signs of resemblance to Danny Redfearn. He smiled at her, and said, 'If I had a sister I guess I'd really like one like you.'

CHAPTER SIX

THEY talked more next day, as the boys weren't doing anything until evening. But after that one candid comment, Bas decided that he had talked enough about himself. He got on well with Matthew, but, as Bas pointed out, they would probably never meet again. So, 'No point in going on about the past. Be realistic, man. Life is odd. Take the bad times, and enjoy the good times. And don't let it get to you!'

'And that's your advice? Sooner said than done.' Susanna felt sad, that such a young kid could advise her.

'You have to be strong, Sue. In the end, who is there but yourself you can rely on?' He said it coolly, in his gentle unassuming way.

'Well—friends? Parents? You've got Ma and Say Lun as well as us.'

'I know that. And I'm grateful. But you know I wouldn't burden you with my affairs.'

'Well that's wrong of you, because I'd like to help. If ever you need anyone, I mean,' she added swiftly. The young animal could still take fright. 'I don't even know your surname.'

'Well, you won't have trouble remembering it. It's Smith.'

'I hope you won't take off again without saying *au revoir*.'

'Thanks. But I think I'll stick around for a while. I'm getting the taste for Singapore nightclubs. I'll be popping in to say hello.'

'Good.' She said it firmly, hoping that he knew she meant it.

'By the way, Matt—hope you're free Sunday night. They want a spare drummer at the Phoenix. I said you were the best.'

'Thanks anyway. But aren't we going out, Sue? Gerry Sovani's taking us?'

'Oh, that'll be okay. You'll be back from an old folks' party in time for the Phoenix. Things don't liven up till after two.'

'Meet you back here then.'

'Okay. Elevenish.'

It was refreshing to dress up for Gerry's evening. There was no quibble about what to wear. It was quite simple. Gerry just expected all his girlfriends to look as though they had just stepped off the cover of American *Vogue*. So it was a case of pulling all the stops out, and knowing that it was impossible to go over the top.

So when the doorbell rang on Sunday evening, Susanna answered it looking cool and classically elegant in a dark green silk dress that hugged her figure, yet showed off her slim neck and upswept white-gold hair with an off-the-shoulder neckline. He stood back, admiring, and there was no doubt it was a nice feeling, to be admired and appreciated. No snide remarks about false dignity, no comments that upset her steady familiar way of thinking tonight.

'This is my brother.'

Matt shook hands. 'It's very thoughtful of you to ask me.' He was tidy, hardly smart compared with Gerry, but passable. 'Would you like a drink before we go?' They had specially bought some white wine, and remembered to put it in the fridge.

'I think not. Thank you, but I am driving this evening.'

'What car have you?' Matt was car crazy, and it transpired that Gerry knew a lot about them too, so the journey to the leafy suburbs in the long shining Mercedes was passed with enthusiastic exchange of facts about '0 to 60', 'petrol injection' and 'turbo powered'.

But Matt was a sociable lad, and as they were introduced to the quietly upper-class Indian family, his face lit up at the sight of the two daughters of the house, and they were soon chatting about pop music in a corner, with a tape recorder that must have cost as much as a small car. Demure and gently-spoken, the sari-clad girls showed a very thorough knowledge of all the latest charts, and the younger one unearthed some tatty magazines from underneath a spotless onyx table. It broke the ice at once, and Susanna soon felt at home in the type of luxury she dreamed of sometimes.

Wine and drinks were handed round on silver trays. 'Please, do use the garden if you wish.' Mr Mattiar was only too happy to hear the appreciative comments about the house. 'I have installed some sonic devices which are supposed to keep insects away. So you should not be bothered.'

Gerry said quietly, 'I am sorry, Susanna. I have not had time to speak to you at all. I did not mean to be rude.'

'You haven't been. You've been very nice to Matt. This is an evening he'll remember for a long time.'

'So will the girls, I think. He has even taken their attention from me.'

'You don't mind?'

'Susanna, you know me better than that, surely. Delightful girls they may be, but hero worship is a little trying. Now if they took your attention from me, I would be very angry indeed.'

'I've never seen you angry. Not even a little ruffled.'

'I hope you do not. I am not proud of being quick tempered. But I try to keep calm at work. My patients would not be too happy if I told them what I really thought of them sometimes.'

'I know how you feel.'

'You like Tilly working with you? She is a very competent woman.'

Susanna didn't reply at once. She sipped her drink, and looked out over the smooth moonlit lawn. She didn't want to sound petty-minded. Better not to say anything.

She felt Gerry's hand rest on her bare shoulder, and caress it very lightly. 'Something is worrying you?'

'Sorry. I didn't mean to be moody. I—to be honest, Gerry, I have this feeling that she's enjoying the Pagoda so much—I'll lose my job.'

'Surely not. You do it too well. And you are theatre sister also. She can't take that away.'

'I know it sounds silly. But the Pagoda sort of—belongs to me. I can't bear the thought of not being part of it.'

'That's life, Susanna. Even for a great big dentist. One day the Pagoda will have to carry on without me. But I understand how you feel. You have worked very hard to help to make it a success.'

'I feel much better for talking about it. Thanks for listening.'

'Susanna.' A shrill voice. Her hostess. 'Do let me introduce you to our other guests. You have met Mr Singh? And Mr and Mrs Yu?' Susanna was separated from Gerry for a while. She chatted dutifully with the guests, mostly middle-aged and very affluent. She had not seen so many glittering diamonds outside a shop window before.

'Excuse me, but you're Susanna, aren't you?' She turned to look up into the handsome face of an Indian girl a little older than herself, in a gown that looked as though it came direct from Paris, sheer silk, in voluminous folds, showing off a tiny waist with a wide glittering belt. 'I'm Indrani. Gerry's sister. Didn't he tell you we'd be here?'

'No. How very nice.' Susanna shook her hand. 'You live in Singapore?' It was a bit of a shock. Surely he should have told her, if he knew his sister would be here.

'Actually, Mother lives in New Delhi. I'm based in Paris at the moment. After I finished my language course at the Sorbonne, I had made so many friends, I couldn't bear to leave. Princess Caroline was such fun. But after she went to California, the group broke up a little.'

Susanna was not impressed. She had met boasters before. 'Paris sounds nice. But I like it here.'

Indrani was looking under thick lashes with a very piercing gaze. 'Won't you come and say hello to Mother?'

'Your mother?' Gerry's mother. Susanna felt flustered, but she was fortunately not the type of person to show it. If meeting the sister was a blow, this was even worse. But she pulled herself together rapidly. She had managed the small talk very well so far. 'She is on holiday?'

'Well, I came over to Delhi to see her. But it was even more hot and stuffy there in August, so we decided to pay Gerry a visit. I'm not sure if he was pleased or not.' She put down her tall glass of fruit juice with a grimace. 'God, how I'd love a Pernod. But I don't drink unless I'm in Europe.'

'Honestly? Why?'

'It's the parents. The young people are okay, but many parents like to think they've brought their kids up never to be so fast and sinful.'

'Your mother is a—bit of a dragon, then?'

'I'll say.' Then the girl covered her full red lips with a hand tipped with crimson. 'No, Susanna. Come and meet her. She's a sweetie really.'

Susanna found that the natural anger that came from knowing that she had been brought here without being told who she was to meet quite banished any nervousness she might have had. Indrani went over to a group of ladies in silk saris of varying beautiful shades. She touched the arm of one, who detached herself from the group and walked over, with stately steps. She was slight and thin, but very upright. Her sari was woven through with gold thread, which shimmered in the coloured lights in the trees. She held out her hand in the European tradition, rather than fold her hands together in the typical Indian way. Susanna shook it firmly. 'How lovely to meet you. Gerry didn't tell me you would be here.'

The aquiline face was dark, with a carefully applied spot in the centre of her forehead, and a very large diamond in the left side of her nose. The dark eyes gave nothing away. 'How do you do, Miss Valentine. It is a pleasure. My son has told me about you.'

Susanna wondered what on earth Gerry had said. It would have been decent to tell her first. She took a deep breath. Her small talk had to be expert now. 'We have a very special group at the Pagoda. I am very happy to be a humble part of the set-up. They are all at the top of their professions.'

'So I understand.'

'Perhaps you'd like to see it? I'd be happy to show you round.'

'My stay here is very short, Miss Valentine. But I am grateful for your offer. Your parents are here?'

'No. I came here of my own free will. They weren't too pleased at my decision. But I know I made the right choice.'

'Your father is working still? You are too young for him to be retired.'

So, she was probing into her social class. Finding out if her family were good enough for the Sovanis. Fair enough. 'My father is a schoolmaster. Physics and Chemistry. My mother teaches dancing to little girls in our own home. It's a big old house, and there's room for a dance studio.' She saw the old lady's eyes narrow in approval. For good measure, she added, 'And my brother Matt—have you met him?—is going to study medicine at Edinburgh in October.' There. Socially acceptable? The medicine bit certainly made a good impression. But underneath, Susanna was boiling. How dare he submit her to this cross examination?

Mrs Sovani smiled graciously. 'You come from a very happy family.'

'Yes. Happy but poor. Our riches were in our happiness.' She watched the old lady, waiting for an expression of disapproval. Strange. She thought Indian families were fussy about money.

'How very sweet. Now, if you'll excuse me, I must have a word with Mrs Mettiar.' She smiled. 'I hope we meet again, Miss Valentine.'

'She likes you.' Indrani muttered as her mother left them. 'I say Susanna, you didn't mind, did you?'

Susanna pursed her lips. 'Would you? Being interrogated like prisoner? She sounded like my old headmistress. Or like one of the worst sort of matrons.'

'You passed with flying colours. It would be an ordeal for Mother, of course, if Gerry married outside our caste, never mind our own nationality. But Mother realises that he will not be driven, so she has to allow him to make his own choice now. She has been very brave about it.'

Susanna tossed her head. 'What is this talk of marriage? I'm a colleague of Gerry's, not one of his string of glamour girls. There's no question of anything serious . . .'

'There must be. Otherwise, why did he ask us to meet you?'

'I see.' Somehow the jolly idea that she would be the one to bring the handsome Gerry to the altar had lost its charm. Marrying him would not be gaining a husband, so much as a whole tribe. All worrying about their caste, and their family dignity . . . 'Would I have been any less of a person if my father was in prison for fraud? Or my mother scrubbed steps to send Matt to Medical College?' Her feelings were raw. She was thinking of what Danny had told her—about true dignity of soul requiring no outward demonstration. How very right he was. And she had scorned what he said, distrusting it . . .

'Come on, Susanna. Mother was great. Look how she didn't mind about you having no money.'

Susanna didn't notice what they ate that night. Matthew made up for her lack of interest by his immense appettite and enthusiasm. But she was only relieved when they were in the Mercedes, homeward bound.

'Will you drop me in Orchard Road, please? I'm singing for my supper tonight. Well, drumming.' He was high. 'Those girls were gorgeous.'

'If you can manage any more supper, bring home some Alka Seltzer.' Susanna joked with him, but her feelings were still jangling.

'I'll be pretty late. But I've got the key.'

Gerry drew up at the kerb. He turned off the engine. 'Susanna?'

'Thank you for a lovely evening.' She opened the car door. He was quick to follow her, and lock the car doors.

'I'd better see you up. It's late.'

At the door he opened it and pushed it open for her to enter. Then he followed her, and closed it behind him.

'It's a bit late, Gerry.'

'I'd love a drink, if it's not too much trouble.' And she knew she had to offer some, because they had asked him earlier.

'All right.' She took the bottle from the fridge, her fingers making marks on the frosted surface.

She was struggling with the opener, when he said quietly, 'Let me.' And she was conscious then of the strength in those slim wrists, the dark hairs on the back of his hands, the total helplessness she felt against his tall manliness. He was a gentleman, she knew, but now she was seeing another side of him—determined, unwilling to be crossed, and strong in his desires. She winced as he wrenched the cork from the bottle. He poured two glasses with practised ease. And she watched the taut muscles in his forearms with apprehension. He tossed off the wine, and refilled his own glass. She saw something in his dark eyes that was new, raw. He was a caged tiger, this his animal side, the passionate and lustful Gerry who would not be easily denied . . .

'What's the matter, Susanna? Won't you drink to us?' His voice was deceptively gentle. She wondered whether to be ashamed of her unkind thoughts. 'Your hand is shaking. Shall I turn off the fan?'

She shook her head, and put the glass down untasted in case she spilt wine on her dress. 'I'm tired, Gerry. It was a nice dinner, but I hadn't expected to be vetted like that.'

'I'm so sorry.' His voice was now melting honey. 'I meant no harm. I only knew myself that they were coming three days ago.'

'It's okay now. Forget it.'

'You're not frightened of me, are you?'

She tried to be logical. She wasn't frightened of old Gerry, of course not. Yet he was somehow very different tonight. She replied carefully, 'No, I don't think so. But I am of myself. I'm a bit unsure of my own feelings tonight.'

He drained his wine, and set the glass down. Then he slowly turned her to face him. She was glad to see that the tiger-light had gone from his eyes. It was 'her' Gerry again, the one she was almost in love with. The threat had receded. Even though his hands held her by the shoulders, the touch was gentle again. Then he said, 'I'm glad, Susanna. Few girls these days hold back from making love. It adds to your specialness. Friends?'

She tried to keep her voice steady at his words. 'Yes, of course.' She felt terribly unsophisticated, but at that moment it didn't matter all that much.

'And you do like me a little, darling, in spite of what I put you through at the party?' He put one dark hand lightly under her chin, so passionless now, that he might almost have been going to give her an injection before a filling.

'I do. Yes.' Her heart felt as though it was fibrillating. Why?

'Good.' His arm went round her terribly gently. As he tightened his hold, her trembling lessened, and she felt trust in his gentleness. He bent and kissed her forehead, his warm lips lingering on her eyelashes, and then slowly finding her mouth, and holding it without aggression. Gently, so gently. It was almost beautiful really. What a good feeling it was, being held like this, as though prized and desired . . . There was no return of the earlier panic now. With this Gerry, she didn't mind losing a little control of her own will, and she lifted her face fractionally, increasing the pressure of her lips on his. As though she had given a signal, she felt the muscles tense in his arms and in his back, and she was drawn very close, yielding and willing against him. Susanna forgot time.

Vaguely into her dream came voices. Voices outside on the stairs. Gerry drew away. 'Someone's coming.' And into the incessant chirping of the night crickets came men's voices in cheerful dialogue.

'It's Matthew. And Bas, I think.'

'Your brother?'

'Yes.'

'They are coming in?'

'Oh yes.'

And in seconds the key was heard in the lock, and footsteps were approaching. Susanna hastily put on the small lamp, and pushed back her dishevelled hair. 'Hello boys.'

'Hi Sue. Hello Dr Sovani.' Matthew's open face showed no sign of embarrassment. 'Bas and I'd like some cocoa, if that's okay. Like some?'

Susanna turned to introduce Bas to Gerry, but the man was already at the door, his eyebrows betraying more than mild irritation. 'See you tomorrow, Susanna.'

She followed him to the door. She was torn between relief and slight disappointment. 'Good night, Gerry.'

The boys were chatting in the kitchen, but Susanna didn't join them. It had been a traumatic night. She overheard scraps of their conversation as she fell asleep . . .

'You were good, you know—dead good. We could get a real band going if you weren't going back to rotten old University.'

Susanna held her breath. Please don't let Matt be tempted. Bas was a nice boy—but not a good influence. But she needn't have feared. 'Tell you what Bas, keep in touch. I'll come out and work at the Pagoda and we can form a new group—Dr Valentine and the—the Love Birds.'

'You really want to do it, don't you? Medicine?'

'You bet. And not just for an Aston Martin.' There was a silence for a while, and Susanna pictured Bas looking waiflike. Matt was philosophical. 'There's so many lousy things people do, man—making bombs to kill people, or pesticides to poison the air they breathe. I'd like to do a bit on the other side—not much, but better than jumping on someone's head, isn't it?'

'Yeah.' Silence for a while, then he said, 'I'd better get back to the Mings.'

'It's late man. Stay here. Sue won't mind if you have the sofa. Sue!'

Susanna replied with a muffled shout. 'Perfectly all right, Bas.' And then something clicked in her mind. Mings . . . that must be Ma and Say Lun. Would they by any chance have something to do with the poor woman Danny was operating on next morning? Somehow, the pieces were fitting together, like a puzzle. She must ask Bas tomorrow . . . Somewhere in the weary jungle of her mind was a tiny jewel of relief that she hadn't lost her virginity to Gerry. Because she knew she didn't love him enough.

She was late waking up, and almost ran to work in the clear morning sun. She didn't bother to put up her hair, but tied it with a narrow ribbon. It was Mrs Ming's day, and she would already have had her premed. Both the boys were fast asleep, and she didn't wake them. She enjoyed being in theatre—apart from the fact that Tilly Paw couldn't steal that side of her job, it was rewarding to work with 'her' doctors as a colleague. They knew each other's technique, and Phil Chan hardly ever had to ask Susanna for anything, knowing that she would have it almost before he realised he needed it. Danny would not be disappointed in her, she knew. And at least in theatre, Tilly Paw could be as cute as anything, but she was totally unnecessary to requirements. In spite of her rush, Susanna found herself humming. She was looking forward to seeing Danny again. She had missed the cheery banter, the warmth of his voice and the light in his eyes. Three things that would still be obvious, even if everything else was hidden by hospital gown and mask.

The tumour had not been easy. At first there was no problem. The bone was removed cleanly, and a mass removed from the frontal cavity. But then Danny snorted, 'Sister, my head,' and she had to grab a tissue before his increasing perspiration blinded him at a tricky moment.

The assistant surgeon, Jim Nye, was giving him every encouragement, his own ego greatly boosted by working actually with the Great Man. 'That's amazing, sir. We won't need to take any more vessels. She's been a lucky woman.'

Danny snorted again, most unlike him. 'Look here. The damn thing is stuck—grown into the bone. I'm going to have to leave it. Can't risk fracturing that. Here, Sister—' he extended the forceps towards Susanna— 'get that to Histology pronto.' He dropped a small piece of the bone into the bowl she held. She handed it wordlessly to the nurse, who nodded, and scampered out.

'Okay. Drainage tube.' He was closing the skin now.

'Will she recover her memory?'

'There's every chance. Depends how well the brain expands again, now that it's got its own space back.' He finished the final stitch, and Susanna took the suture needle from him. He stretched his arms and back. Then he drew the back of his hand wearily across his forehead. He had been working for five hours. 'She's been taking the anti-convulsants?'

'Yes, Dr Redfearn.'

'Okay. I'll go and see her when she's back in the ward.' The still recumbent lady was wheeled away, with Susanna supervising her oxygen mask and saline drip, while the other nurse kept an eye on the various drainage tubes. Her colour was good.

In the ward, Susanna took her blood pressure once again and tested all four limbs for movement and power. They all moved, and she sighed with relief. If they found out that she lived alone, at least she would not be paralysed. Susanna shone a torch into her blearily open eyes. 'Hello, my dear. Everything went well. You know what day it is?'

'Yes.'

'And where you are?'

'Susanna, you've been so good to me. I'll never forget the Pagoda.'

'Don't try to talk just yet. Your memory will soon be clearer.'

'It's better already. I don't feel that fuzziness any more.'

'That is wonderful. Get some sleep now.'

It had been a long morning, but Susanna didn't want to leave until she was sure she left her patient well. 'Sister Valentine, don't you want to go for some lunch?'

'Later.' The adrenalin was still keeping her alert. She monitored her patient for another hour before she felt her eyes closing and the stress of the morning, plus last night's lateness, begin to tell. She forced herself upright. There was a slight leak of blood from under the tight head bandage. She reached for a sterile pad to mop it away.

At that moment, she heard Danny Redfearn's voice at the ward door. She started up, and the edge of the pad dislodged the entire drainage tube, so that the contents spilled over the pillow and the patient's face. He was at the bedside in a second. 'Dammit. That's all I need!' His face grimaced in annoyance. Susanna was mortified. But she was sensible enough not to make things worse by apologising. She swiftly pulled the emergency trolley towards him, while he unwrapped the compression bandage, and re-inserted the tube between the stitches. His breathing was laboured, showing his anger at having to redo it. She felt ashamed of her untypical clumsiness, due particularly to her tiredness. But it should not have happened. Redfearn said nothing to her as he replaced the bandage, and then pulled the blanket up to her neck, and patted her shoulder. 'Keep an eye on her temperature.'

Then he left the ward at a rate of knots, with Jim Nye and Jo-Jo close behind. Susanna sat down again, her face pink with embarrassment. She ought not to have let that happen. Could it have been her sudden intake of breath as she heard Danny's voice. Did a man's mere arrival cause her such physical clumsiness? She took out the thermometer and the sphygmomanometer and monitored again with extra-careful fingers. The hospital was hushed as most patients slept. She might have been the only living thing on the entire planet, except for the distant hum of traffic, and the occasional sleepy chirrup of the sparrows outside the open window in the heavy afternoon heat.

'Are you asleep, Valentine?' The longed-for voice drifted into her dreams, and she smiled as she slept. Then she sat up with a start. Danny stood there—in the flesh. She looked about her. Another nurse had quietly taken over the monitoring instruments. She stood up. Together they walked out of the hospital wing and into the garden, saying nothing. They stopped at the place where they had talked last time. This time they were both on the same side of the bridge. 'I was disgustingly rude to you Valentine.'

'I was a clumsy oaf.'

His hand touched her loose hair, untidy as she had not combed it after changing from theatre gear. 'Nothing will excuse my sheer barbarity.'

'Forget it. Please.'

'If you'll have dinner with me, I might be able to.'

'Danny, you don't have to . . .'

'Oh but I do. I must.' He smiled, and let his hand fall from her hair. 'Some things just have to be, Valentine.'

CHAPTER SEVEN

HE was a strange man. Simple words—some things just have to be. No more. After that, they both went back to their work, and Susanna tried not to allow the words to turn to a magic Irish spell in her brain. But it wasn't only the words—it was the nearness of the man, and the direct look in his lovely eyes, crinkly at the corners, and so very sincere. At the time, was this the way he spoke to the other girls? And did their knees turn to water the way hers did? Well, she would do her best to ignore the whole thing. Best just to get on with her work. That is, provided that Tilly Paw didn't interfere too much in that.

Fortunately, she didn't come in at first, getting her father's secretary to telephone and say that Miss Paw had flown to Tokyo last night with her father, and would not be back till next day. Good. Tuesday would then be a nice normal day—unless Dr Redfearn came round wielding any more charm. But he didn't. He was busy too. And as Susanna sat in the office with Mei Li at lunchtime, it all felt deliciously ordinary again.

'Is her memory coming back? May I call and see her?'

'She hasn't remembered anything yet. I'll see this evening when I visit. But Danny doesn't want too many people questioning her. She seems to trust me as a friend, so he's asked me to chat normally with her, and question her only gently. You see, if I asked any leading questions, she might think she remembered, but I would have put the idea in her head.'

'Sure. I can see that.' Mei Li finished her fairy cake and got rid of the crumbs on her simple white cheongsam. 'But you mentioned you had met someone called Ming in Changi?'

'Yes. They run a café. But I've no idea how to find the place again. Bas took us, and he ran down a lot of side streets. I never even looked at the names.'

'I met Bas yesterday with your brother. Scruffy little chap, isn't he? But that thin type often turn into attractively quiet men, who can use their little-boy looks to charm the leaves from the trees.'

'Mei Li! I don't know how you learnt so much about the opposite sex. You don't go out with men.' Susanna didn't want to tell her friend about her suspicions about Bas yet. But it was a coincidence that she had described Bas growing up like Danny Redfearn.

They went back to work, and Jo-Jo and Phil Chan came in from lunch. 'I'll go to Changi and try to find that place, if Bas doesn't turn up to take me in the next couple of days,' promised Susanna.

Mrs Ming was lying flat and thin under the sheet. But at the sight of Susanna that evening, she sat up at once. Her eyes brightened, and she held out a hand to hold Susanna's. 'My name is Lucy Ming. I know where I live, Susanna. At least, I remember what it looks like.'

'That is wonderful. Is it all right for you to sit up?'

'Oh yes. Dr Redfearn has seen me, and is very pleased. He told me all about the operation, and I do remember having this fuzzy feeling in my head, and going to my own doctor for advice.'

'Yes? Who is your doctor?'

'I'm not sure of his name. But I am a teacher, you know. I teach juniors at Fraser Street. Only I still can't quite remember everything. I can see some of my pupils in my mind's eye.' Her smile came back. 'Dr Redfearn said I mustn't worry, because my brain would recover in time.'

'Where is Fraser Street?'

'I'm sorry. I can't just think . . .'

'Please don't worry, Lucy. I'll look it up.' Susanna wondered whether to question her more. She seemed well enough, but she didn't want to upset her. So just one more enquiry. 'You said something about a bridge —or a Bridget? It wouldn't be your doctor's name—or headmistress?'

She wrinkled her forehead under the swathe of bandages. And only one side of her forehead wrinkled. 'What are you smiling at?'

Susanna picked up the hand mirror, and showed her. 'What a lucky woman. You won't get wrinkled when you are old.' And at Lucy's request she drew a little diagram, to show which muscle and nerves had had to be severed to remove her tumour. 'Don't worry. You can get along without them perfectly well. And you'll only age on one half.' They both laughed and made fun of the situation, and it was good to see the genuine clarity of thought that had come back to Lucy Ming.

'I'm thirty-seven.' She made the announcement suddenly.

'Would you like me to go and check up on the school tonight? You could have some relatives worrying about you?'

She shook her head. 'No I live alone. I have a very nice bungalow—small, but just what I need for myself.' She looked up again. 'What was it you said about a bridge?'

But Susanna saw she had taxed her enough. 'Don't give it another thought. Maybe in the morning more things will come back.' She made Lucy lie back, and in spite of her recent animation, the patient's eyes closed almost immediately. Yes, Danny had told them that craniotomy patients tended to be exceptionally sleepy. She left the ward, glad to have gained something more from her slowly improving memory.

Next day was disappointing, because Lucy was feeling too sleepy to talk, and there was some swelling over one side of her face. Susanna decided at once that rest was what she needed, and after leaving her a small bunch of spider-orchids, she patted the thin hand and left her to sleep.

She paused as she returned to the foyer. Mei Li had already gone home, and in the dental section, Amanda had covered her typewriter and put the magazines away. It was quiet but for the tinkling of the water from the little fountain—and a murmur of voices by the door behind a potted palm. It was Tilly. And Danny. In very close conversation. The sight annoyed her—probably because she had remembered his last sweet words to her—and he didn't mean them. He was an inveterate ladies' man, and couldn't help doing it. But it hurt. She turned, intending to go out through the hospital exit, rather than pass the whispering couple. Tilly's body language was very obvious, her slim waist pushed towards Danny. She wore a very pretty flowery dress with a full skirt that brushed against him. He was bending down to her, his expressive hand occasionally moving against the honey-coloured arm, lingering there as he spoke.

Retreating as quietly as she could, Susanna opened the door to the Japanese garden. But it rattled as she turned the knob. 'Valentine!' The imperious summons. There was an element of urgency in his voice, and as she turned, he was already coming towards her, holding out both hands in a gratifying manner. 'You've talked to her?' Powerless to resist him, and knowing what it meant to him, Susanna forgot her intention to creep away. She waited until Danny reached her. Tilly walked after him, the skirt of her dress swinging gently in the flow of the air-conditioning. She was off-hand, but she definitely didn't want to miss anything important.

'Lucy's memory is coming back. You haven't seen her?' asked Susanna.

'I have. She's got a bit of CSF leakage. If it doesn't settle by tomorrow, I'll do a lumbar puncture. But I didn't talk to her about herself, Susanna. I'm leaving that to you. You have her confidence.' And Susanna felt as though he'd said something beautiful. He had called her by her name, instead of the jokey 'Valentine' that showed he was only playing with her. And the way he said it made it such a sweet-sounding name, that she thought she had never liked it until now.

'She has no relatives. She lives alone in a bungalow, and she's thirty-seven. She's a schoolteacher.'

'How absolutely wonderful.' Danny visibly relaxed.

Tilly said sweetly, 'Have you asked her how much money she has? Some teachers do quite well.'

Danny said quietly, his eyebrows showing disapproval, 'You don't mean that.'

She flicked lightly at her dress. 'Perhaps I don't if you say so darling. But it is going to matter, isn't it?'

Susanna said, 'I've got the name of the school. I was wondering if we should find out where it could be tonight.'

She had the name written down. As she passed it to Danny, it was Tilly who flicked it from his hand, and looked at it with cool interest. 'I know Singapore better than you, darling. I'll find your Fraser Street for you.' She was right of course. She had lived here all her life. 'I'd like to have the proper address.'

Danny stood slightly aloof. 'So that you can send her the bill?' His voice was still quiet, his eyes so clearly scornful.

'Naturally. That would set my mind at rest.'

Susanna thought of the poor spinster lying under her sheet, her head swathed with bandages, and aching with the swelling. And she felt a great anger against Tilly

Paw. Her banter was cruel, her beautiful eyes cold. How could someone as warm as Danny Redfearn even hang about with her? Yet one look at her dainty little figure in its exquisite clothes was enough to answer that question. Danny had his principles. But he was only human.

Danny said, 'Well, once the stitches come out, I'll let her go home if she's got a maid. So she won't be a thorn in your pretty side any more.'

'She can come to my place. I told you. It's handy —and my maid will come in every day if I ask her.'

His eyes lost their coldness when he looked at Susanna. 'Thanks.'

Tilly said, 'My dear, what a ministering angel we are.' Then she turned to Danny, ignoring Susanna completely. 'Well, is it the Raffles or not? Ahmed can take us in the Mercedes. I want to go on with my proposition. And I'm also dying for a drink.'

Susanna didn't wait to hear any more about what proposition had been made to Danny. She didn't want to see the man she admired follow slavishly what this little Chinese harpy ordered. She went past them quickly, and ran down the steps into the fresh warm night air. There was a huge moon just coming up over the rooftops, glowing orange in the misty afterglow of the sunset. It was good to see something natural and beautiful, after the narrow egotism of her employers' pretty little daughter.

But the daughter was efficient enough to present her with the address of Fraser Street School on Thursday morning. And Susanna for once was glad Tilly was there to deputise for her, as she took the afternoon off to take the bus for Changi. As she sat in the sleek silver coach, enjoying the breeze when it went fast between stops, she wondered if there really could be any connection between the Mings that Bas knew, and Lucy. They both lived in Changi.

One question Lucy had already answered. She had gone to her doctor about her headaches. So she was not seeking Danny Redfearn out because she wanted to give him some secret message, that was for sure. She was coming to him because he was a neurologist and she needed one. No mystery there.

The headmistress at Fraser Street was relieved to see Susanna, and hear about Lucy Ming. She confirmed that she taught there, and gave her the address of the little bungalow not far from the school. The head was a tiny birdlike woman, with a habit of putting her head on one side. But she had a powerful voice, and was clearly instantly obeyed in the school.

Susanna said, knowing it was a question she had to ask, 'Do you have anyone called Bridget here?'

'Bridget? My, that's a long time ago. Yes. I recall Bridget Smith. Yes, she was friendly with Lucy—as much as she was friendly with anyone. She was a quiet strange woman. She taught well, but had a lonely life, just herself and a small son. He went off with relatives when she died. I always thought her death was a mistake, not deliberate.'

Susanna's heart quickened. 'Deliberate?'

'Overdose, sleeping pills. She was rather neurotic. But I always maintained that it was a mistake. It is easy to take another lot when you are already a bit sleepy and cannot remember the last dose. Yes. The verdict was accidental death, and I agree with it.' And she nodded her little head again. 'Lucy found her. Perhaps that was something that stuck in her memory. Well, let me know how she gets on—if there's anything her colleagues can do. We'll visit, of course.'

Susanna said, 'The Hospital is rather expensive . . .'

The little headmistress smiled. 'Don't worry about your fees. Lucy is extremely careful. She was well-insured, I promise you. The policies will be at her bank in Changi. Shall I see about them for her?'

Susanna sat in a small café in Siong Lim Avenue drinking iced lemonade. Miss Ming was indeed the friend of Bridget Smith/Redfearn. Yet she had come to see Danny about her own personal problem. She probably had never even heard the name Redfearn before, and it must have meant nothing to her, except as a consultant who could help her with her medical troubles. It was too much of a coincidence. She had to find out more. Yet who was there but Lucy herself? The answers were locked up in her memory, and were coming to light so very slowly.

Her one chance was to find the Ming's café. Ma and Say Lun would know. They were so fond of Bas, that it was likely that they were the 'relatives' who took him in after his mother died. If only she had made a note of the street where the café was. She asked the proprietor when she paid her bill for the lemonade. He laughed. 'Changi not a village any more. Not since airport come here. Whole city.' He shook his head. 'Only chance is if they got a telephone. You ring them and see.'

'Thanks.' But she already knew they had no phone. Every Ming in the book had been contacted before the operation. She walked back to the bus station, frustrated and very hot. She stood for a while, trying to recall where they had jumped off the bus, running like children along the narrow streets and alleys. Weary though she was, she walked around the area for a while, tripping on uneven cobbles, and sweating as she climbed up the airless streets. But nowhere did she find a basement that looked like the Mings. And people she asked only shook their heads and couldn't help.

The Pagoda was closing when she got back. She asked Rahman if Danny were in. 'I don't see him go.' So she entered the quiet foyer again, and went over to her own phone to buzz his rooms. 'Danny?'

'Hello, Sue. You've found out anything?' It was Tilly in his room again. She really had got her claws into the man.

Susanna didn't know if Tilly knew his secrets or not, but she didn't intend to tell them over the phone. So she merely said, 'No relatives. But well-insured.'

'Very good. Excellent detective work, Sue.' Then she said, 'By the way, we're still a bit tied up here. But I'd better let you know that Danny is going over to our Hospital in Brunei next week. I've cancelled his appointments.'

'Brunei?' Susanna squeaked the word in amazement. What was the woman up to now?

'Yes. We haven't got a neurologist on the staff, and there are a few patients Dr Nanda wants him to see. So we're flying out on Sunday.'

'Right.' Susanna replaced the phone. If Danny couldn't even pass on his own messages, then she didn't want to speak to either of them. She realised she'd been toiling around in the heat, while they'd been lounging in his rooms, passing the time together no doubt to their mutual satisfaction. The more she thought, the angrier she got. Grabbing her bag, she was ready to storm out of the building. Rahman already stood at the door, dangling the keys.

As she took one last look round—her tidy habits didn't go away just because she was annoyed—she saw that Gerry's door was partly open, and her methodical mind wouldn't let her go until she'd closed it. She smiled wanly at his empty surgery, the pale blue furnishings and the restful picture of a seascape to take the patients' minds off their teeth. Gerry had been polite since that evening together, but had not prolonged any conversations with her. And she didn't mind. She had seen the streak of self-will under his veneer of calm—the quiet determination to get his own way in everything. She was relieved that things had gone no further. She patted a speck of dust from one of his rubber plants, and closed the door softly, with no regrets.

Lucy was much better tonight. She did remember most of what Susanna had found out. And she remembered Bridget too. 'Of course. She was a very quiet person. She said her life in England had been a failu.e.' Then she added, 'I did miss her. I think I was her only friend.'

As though starting a new topic, Susanna said, 'You heard of Dr Redfearn through your own doctor, you said?'

'Yes. He said my headaches needed a second opinion, and that a famous neurologist had newly come to Singapore. So I decided to see him.'

'Even though you had never heard the name before?'

'Redfearn. I'm sure I would have remembered that. Although he does say that my brain could go on adapting to having its space back for up to three months.'

'Yes.' Anyway, it didn't really matter. Bridget had died, and Bas was all right. What more could Danny want to know? 'Is Ma Ming your relative?'

'Ma is my cousin. I must write to her. We weren't close. She isn't on the phone.'

'I'll take a message if you like.'

'No, never mind. She's a busy woman, and not too good a walker. There's no need for her to come and see me. I'll just let her know I'm all right.'

'Lucy, what happened to Bridget's child?'

'She made some sort of will making sure that his father couldn't have any legal claim on him. The lawyers said he would go to a children's home. I don't think we saw him again, but they told me he had settled down there.' She thought for a moment. 'This is all so long ago. I'd forgotten poor Bridget almost. The boy must be grown-up now.'

'Yes.'

It was late. The crickets were noisy tonight in the Japanese garden. She sat on the wall, and just let the sound shrill all around her. She didn't know what to feel, what to do. In the middle of the turmoil of the city, this was a quiet and tranquil spot. Perhaps some of its tranquillity would help the turmoil in her own mind.

She heard the click of the door. But there was no further sound for a while, and Susanna didn't take any notice. Then she heard the click of a pebble on the stone path. She looked up then. He was standing opposite to her, and in the dusk she could see his head was bent, almost in resignation. She tried to summon up the annoyance about Brunei. But annoyance wouldn't come. 'I've been talking to Lucy,' he said.

'So have I.'

'She told me what she told you.' His voice was lifeless. 'She didn't know why you asked her about me.'

'No point.'

'I know.'

They didn't speak for a while. Susanna stayed on the wall, looking down at the stream, at the way the ripples caught the orangeness of the moon. Then he said, as though talking to himself, 'I shouldn't have told anyone why I came. I shouldn't have involved you.'

'It doesn't matter.'

'It does really. You—somehow you seem to have taken it to heart too. I didn't mean to—use you—force you to trail around after me as you did. I didn't think there were women like you in the world.'

It was a compliment—but it didn't cheer her. 'What are you going to do now?'

'I don't know. This is a nice place—but it isn't home. I am not sure that I know where home is any more. Maybe I'll try Australia. I've been invited to lecture in Melbourne.'

She didn't reply. Melbourne, Brunei—what difference did it make? She thought of Bas, his wary eyes, his restless self-assurance . . . It wouldn't help Danny at all, to tell him about this boy. Yet surely it was her duty? Which of them needed her loyalty most? Danny needed to find his son. But if it was Bas, then he had no feelings towards his father. It would be cruel to see the disappointment.

'I'd better go. Matthew might want something.'

'I'll walk along with you.'

She made no comment, though she wondered how Tilly had allowed him to get away tonight. Their apartment blocks were in the same direction. It seemed logical to walk together. They said little. They did not touch as they walked through the loud, happy streets. Danny lingered at the entrance to the temple, and looked up at the garish scarlet and gold painted gates, with the carved lions guarding each side. Their mouths gaped open, showing wonderfully red gullets and glittering pointed teeth.

At her block, they stopped. He looked down at her, and there was the faintest sign of a crinkle back at the corner of his eyes. 'Like some dinner, Valentine?'

'I'm not hungry.'

'I owe you a dinner—for shouting at you on Monday.'

She looked up into his eyes. Somehow she felt very close to him. 'It's all right. It's not important to me. Shouting—compliments—it's all part of life. And I really am not hungry.'

His face changed. It suddenly seemed important to him. 'Please? I—'

There was a sudden intrusion of running footsteps coming very fast. The stopped close by the couple in the shadows. 'Sue? Is that you?'

She turned. It was Matthew, and Bas was with him. They were breathless and cheerful. 'Hello you two. Go on up. You've got the key.'

'Thanks. Bit of a rush actually. Came for the guitar. We've got a gig—a real good one.' He paused, realising that he was being slightly rude. 'Evening, sir.'

Susanna said, 'This is Matt. He'd love to stop and talk about Medical School, but obviously tonight's employment is rather urgent.' She included Bas in her smile. 'And this is Bas, Danny. I think it's short for Basil, but he never told me.' She held her breath as the two faced each other.

The boy grinned, his curls falling over his face almost hiding his eyes. 'It's Sebastian actually. But it doesn't exactly go with my image. Excuse us.' And the lads ran off upstairs, talking excitedly.

Sebastian. Of course. There was no further doubt now, was there? C.C. had said the name, that first evening in his garden, the night Danny had called her the girl with the flaxen hair . . . She turned to him, feeling his feelings as though she could touch them. He stood silent, motionless, turned to stone. She said softly, 'Sebastian?'

Very slowly he nodded. 'I must speak to him.' His voice seemed to come from very deep in his chest.

'Shall we go up?'

He was suddenly nervous, trying to pull himself together. She didn't force him. Then all at once the boys came running down again, slightly cleaner, in different shirts, Bas clutching his beloved guitar. She whispered urgently, 'Don't be scared.' She said to Matt, 'Mind if we come too?'

'Honestly? You want to bring a respectable medical man to a dive in Chinatown?'

Danny spoke. 'I've had a sheltered life, Matt. What's the name of this dive? Do they take credit cards?' He was smiling at them, but Susanna saw the way he looked at the boys, trying to sound casual.

'The Pink Panther. But it's a bit rough, Dr . . . ?'

'Redfearn.'

Bas was scanning Danny's face now, as though something in his voice had set off some old memories. Susanna felt a great well of pity for them both. Was the gulf too wide, or could they bridge it.

But at the name, Bas leapt like some young antelope. 'Have to get going. See you.' He made for a passing cab, and Matthew could do nothing but chase after him. The cab took off again into the moving stream of traffic. As they watched it, Danny's arm went around Susanna, and they stood holding each other very tight. Her ear was close to his heart. She felt it thumping, and sensed the pain that was in it.

She loosened his grip, and took his hand. 'Come on.' She led him up. He sat on a chair while she opened a bottle of wine, and placed a glass by his hand. He watched her, his green eyes suspiciously bright. She put the glass into his hand. Only then did he seem to come to life. He sipped the wine, running his tongue around his lips.

'Tell me about him. How long . . . ? You knew?'

Susanna explained how Matthew had teamed up with Jake and Bas in Sydney. As she spoke, she found herself praising them, their good sense, their certainty of what they wanted in life, their ability to cope.

'Does he take drugs?'

'Bas? Never.'

'You sound as though you're fond of him.'

'I am. He's so wise. When I asked them all one night, they laughed at me. They told me that if they want to live off their wits, it would be pretty daft to go and blunt them with any sort of drug. They hardly drink either. I've only seen them with a beer once. They live on coffee and tea. And cocoa after a tiring gig.'

'Has he never mentioned his family?'

'Briefly.'

'Me?'

Susanna knew how the words would hurt. She tried to put it as gently as she could. 'He's obviously been told that his father didn't care for him or his mother.'

'Obviously.' He finished the wine. 'He got suspicious, didn't he? Just now? When he ran off as though I was trying to shoot him?'

'I think so. I think he knew your voice, even before he heard your name.'

He sat still. Susanna's tender heart was feeling all what he was feeling for himself. She couldn't just sit there. She went and sat on the arm of the chair. 'Danny, I know, I know.' And she put her arms around him as she would a child.

He turned to her, his arms going round her waist, and buried his head against her breasts. 'You don't know. You're so young. You've never lost anyone.' His words were muffled, his hot breath penetrating the thin stuff of her blouse. Then he kissed her—at first over the blouse, and then pulling it aside, and kissing her skin. His eyes were closed, his grip very tight. Then he laid his cheek against her breast, and murmured her name as though in his sleep.

She got up, and led him to the sofa. She closed the blinds and went to him, taking him again in her arms. There was a great surge of passion welling up in him, and though she only half understood it, she knew she was the only person he had to share it with. And she held him close, loving him, freely giving herself as his hands urgently asked.

There was no word spoken as they came together. And then she was no longer giving, but taking, in a mutual glory of fulfilment and release. But as he sank on her afterwards, his eyes closed, his hair damp over his forehead, he said her name again almost under

his breath. And it filled her already full heart with a
renewed tenderness.

He woke after a while. He lifted his head and looked
into her eyes. She hadn't slept, feeling a strange and
exhilarating strength in her. 'I was going to take you
to dinner.' His voice sounded as though he had a
cold.

She said 'Another time maybe.' It was very quiet, so
calm, with only the swish of the fan in the ceiling.

He stood up, and reached for his clothes. 'May
I . . . ?'

She pointed to the bathroom. He picked up his shirt.
Then he looked closely at it, where a single small drop of
red blood had marked it. 'Susanna?' He looked down at
her very earnestly now, and she sat up, modestly cover-
ing herself with her blouse, and smoothing back her hair.
'Susanna?'

She met his look. 'I'm glad it was you.' It was a
whisper.

He bit at his lip, opened his mouth to speak. She
looked down and picked up her skirt. He shook his head,
and went out of the room, and she heard the shower
turned on. She dressed quickly. Her body felt very alive
and tremulous. She brushed her hair back out of her
eyes, smoothed the cushions, and walked through to the
kitchen. Somehow it seemed too ordinary, filling the
kettle, plugging it in, switching on. She felt as though she
were floating where he had taken her, several feet above
the ground. The full realisation had not yet come to her,
but she knew she would never regret what they had
done.

He came into the kitchen. They went into one
another's arms without a word, standing for a long time
together. 'Why are you in here? We'll go out.'

'No. I've got food. Look—there's chicken ready to
cook. Won't that do?'

He nodded. 'Susanna, I have to explain. I didn't mean—I didn't know—I mean—'

'It's all right, honestly.'

'But—'

'I felt the same.'

A trace of his old look came into his eyes. 'What can I say then?'

'Just bring the rest of the wine in. It'll be a bit warm now.'

'I'll put some ice in it.'

He watched her cooking the chicken, standing by her, so that every time she passed him he stopped her for a kiss. 'Do you mind if I stay until the boys come back? He will come back?'

'He might. He often sleeps on the sofa.'

Susanna's eyes were closing when they finally heard footsteps on the stairs. They both sat up, alert. Matt came in and put the guitar carefully in the corner. Danny said, 'Want cocoa? Susanna left it out for you.'

'No thanks.' He sounded subdued.

Suddenly realising, she said, 'Bas isn't coming, is he?'

Matt didn't reply. Danny said, 'He knew who I was, didn't he?'

Matt faced him then. 'Yes, sir, he did.'

'And he wouldn't come and speak to me?'

'No, sir. Said you'd let them down when they needed you, and that—he didn't need you now.'

'I see.'

Susanna said shrilly, 'You didn't even try to persuade him?'

'Of course I did.' Matthew was angry now. 'I argued with him for ages. He told me to shut up and mind my own business, that I didn't know the first thing about it. Then he ran out. I couldn't find him. He might have gone to Ma's, but I don't know how to find that.'

'I can ask Lucy . . .'

Danny said, 'No, Susanna. What's the point? He knows where I am. He'll come if he wishes. If he doesn't come in the next two days, then I'll be off to Brunei. Knowing that he doesn't want to know me.'

'D'you mind if I go to bed?'

They watched him go, realising that his heart was heavy at the loss of his friend.

Danny turned towards the door. He walked up to it before turning back, with a good attempt at a smile on his face. 'We tried, Valentine. You know we tried.'

'I know.' She had to stop her own lips trembling. Because his smile was not in his eyes.

They stood by the door. 'I feel so completely helpless.' Susanna knew her own face must look as tragic as Danny's.

He shook his head, like a boxer trying to recover from a blow. His arms went around her and his voice was deep and hushed. She held him close, sharing his sorrow. He said, 'You've already been dragged into my troubles enough, my lass. But I—I don't want to leave you yet. Do you understand? It's as though I can't . . .'

There was no need for more. Somehow they didn't need words. Their minds spoke together, and what they sensed was tender, sensitive, imbued with human sympathy and natural affection. She made no protest as he began to walk back towards her bedroom, his arms both around her. She held him close. They turned to each other in the shadows and he bent his face to hers. They lay that night in mutual passion, yet it was also comfort, trust and his own desperate need. And Susanna too learned about her need, and understood that night how fully and sincerely it could be satisfied.

CHAPTER EIGHT

IT was late when she woke next morning, and Danny had gone. The sun was high. Matthew wasn't in the spare room, though an empty mug showed he'd had coffee before he went out. Susanna sat in the cheerful kitchen. She wasn't quite certain how she felt, only that yesterday had been some day.

After sitting for half an hour contemplating the kettle, she decided to switch it on and make tea. Last night—oh last night—Danny Redfearn had been next to her as they washed the dishes together, and made coffee while waiting for the boys to come back. She picked up a mug from the shelf, knowing that the last person to touch it had been Danny . . . What would he be doing now? Certainly not mooning round his kitchen thinking of Susanna Valentine, that was sure. If he wasn't gloomy about Bas, then he'd probably have gone out with the Carltons for a round of golf. C.C. had been a leading member of the opulent Tanah Merah Country Club for many years, the select circle whose entry subscriptions cost more than Susanna earned in a year.

It was a lovely place, peaceful and well laid-out. Danny deserved somewhere like that. He had to relax. His personal trauma must not be allowed to affect his work. Yes, if anyone deserved a round of golf at the Tanah Merah, it was Dr Redfearn that sweet morning.

All the same, when the bell rang, she ran quickly to the door. She tried to hide her disappointment when it was only her maid, Alara. Alara lived close by the Gold Hill Plaza. Her husband sold freshly roasted nuts from a tricycle in the evenings, and Alara worked in the day-

114

time, leaving their small son with his father. 'Come in, Alara. I've not tidied up after my brother, I'm afraid.'

'Is all right. I know the boys. They do not look after themselves. They live like the pigs—until they get girl-friend, lah. Then they change number one quick.'

Susanna decided that the maid could work better without her in the flat and she walked along to the Plaza, idling as though her mind was light and untroubled. The physical impact of her evening with Danny had left her in a strange state of lethargy. She wished she had been at work, where her time would be planned out for her.

Force of habit sent her to the corner table at the Silver Swan Bar, but it was already occupied. She was just turning to find another table when the two occupants called her over. She smiled in astonishment. Matthew, dressed in a smart clean shirt, and with his fair hair brushed very neatly, was sitting opposite Mei Li Tan. 'Where are you going, Sue? Come and join us.'

'I say, are you sure you weren't enjoying a private meeting? I would hate to be a gooseberry,' she teased them, and was teased back. It was the best way to get over a severe case of lovesickness. They ordered ginger beer and ice-cream in tall glasses, and a plateful of Bombay mix noodles. Mei Li was looking like a kid, in pale blue jeans, a checked shirt and an American type baseball cap. Matthew, as always, was proving that he was very cheerful when there were any good-looking girls around, and he was describing English school life in great and lurid detail. Mei Li laughed, and didn't know whether to believe him or not.

'I say, isn't that Dr Redfearn?' Matthew was sitting facing the Plaza, while the girls had their backs to the passing crowds.

Susanna's heart gave a leap. She had been remember-ing the way he had lain in her embrace, holding her as though she were very precious to him. She looked round. 'Yes.' It was Danny all right. And he was strolling along, laughing, with two women, one on each side of him.

Mei Li peeped. 'Typical Danny,' she smiled. 'Surrounded by women. That one in white must be Tilly, surely?'

Susanna said, trying not to sound sour, 'No doubt. Who's the other?'

'New one on me. Looks English. Quite pretty. I like the colour of her dress—a lovely mid-blue. Thai silk, at a guess.'

'You girls are amazing. You'll be telling me where she bought her handbag next.' Matthew took a slurp of his rapidly liquidising ice-cream.

Mei Li giggled. 'Not quite. But I think I've seen a dress like that in Tangs'.'

'Don't stare—please, Matthew.'

'Okay. Don't flap, Sue. I don't care where she got her clothes. I just think it's quite a nice way to spend a morning, in between two pretty women.'

Mei Li looked across at him, forgetting the trio in the square. 'I hope that means that you're a very happy man this morning!'

Susanna said drily, 'I think he means if one of them isn't his big sister.'

'Nonsense.' Matthew reached across and gave her a sticky kiss on the cheek. 'I came to see you, didn't I?' He leaned back in his chair. 'I say, d'you know what I'd be doing if I were at home today? Rowing on the canal. Did I tell you I was in the school "fours", Susanna? We had to go out every Saturday, rain or shine, frost or snow. Break the ice, and remove the dead cats some mornings.' He was aiming at Mei Li again, who still didn't know whether to believe him.

Susanna tried hard not to look. But she was aware that Danny's trio was nearing their pavement table. And amid the hubbub of conversation and the jangle of trishaw bells she knew she could hear his voice, that very relaxed, musical voice, in full swing as he amused his ladies almost as Matthew was doing with Mei Li. She was forgotten. While she allowed herself to moon over him, remembering their union with deep emotion—there was Danny Redfearn out with two more available ladies. She looked down with shame. He had been so plausible last night. It almost appeared that he cared.

'Hello, isn't that Matthew Valentine?' Danny's voice was even nearer now. 'Hi, Matt. Nice to see you.'

Then came Tilly's soprano. 'We haven't got time to stop, Danny dear.'

But Danny had seen Susanna then. And as Matthew waved a cheery greeting, the consultant was already at the table, the two women standing behind him looking not exactly pleased. 'Hello Mei Li. Good morning Valentine.' And his voice changed as he looked at her, losing its easy assurance, softer, nicer . . .

Susanna had to face him then, and she saw the narrowed green eyes were on her, searching her face for some sort of reaction. The sun was hot on them now, evading the shade of the small umbrella in the middle of the table. She met his gaze. For a few seconds the rest of the world vanished for her. Nothing existed but Danny Redfearn—and it was almost as though it felt the same for him.

Except for Tilly. 'Hi, girls.' She was superficially jolly, but it was clear that she had no time for such small fry. 'Sorry to dash away so quickly, but Danny has to do some shopping for Brunei, and we're having lunch with the Carltons in half an hour. At the Country Club, of course. The Carltons always lunch there on Saturdays.'

'Isn't that a bit boring?' Matthew was not impressed. He had stood up politely at the approach of Tilly, and now held out his hand. 'How are you? I'm Sue's brother.'

Tilly shook his hand. 'Tilly Paw.'

Danny introduced the other woman then, as she also held out a hand to the tall young student. 'This is Caroline Moore, from England. Caroline, two of my lovely colleagues from the Pagoda, and Matthew Valentine.'

Tilly tried to speak, but Matthew was again full of enthusiasm. 'You're really going to Brunei, sir? I wish I'd had the chance, but my stay has gone too quickly. Home in a day or two. Which part of the country?'

'Bandar Seri Begawan,' Danny began to answer.

Tilly was slick in continuing, 'The sister hospital to the Pagoda is there. And if we don't get to CYC soon, it will make us very late, and we won't get to the airport on time this evening.'

'Are you going, Miss Moore?' Mei Li noticed a look of disappointment over the handsome brunette's face.

Caroline's voice was very English. 'Afraid not. But I'm looking forward to staying in Danny's apartment. And the Carltons will be showing me around.' She turned to Danny. 'And you do promise to get back the moment you have seen all those boring patients, don't you? I'm dying to show you how my tennis has improved.' Susanna eyed her under lowered lids. Caroline's figure was good, and cleverly shown off by the mid-blue dress. It was clear why she had chosen such a striking colour—it matched her lovely eyes exactly. Susanna recalled that Dr Carlton had mentioned a Caroline at that first party. And now she was staying in Danny's flat . . .

The goodbyes were said in a rush, and Danny was whipped off to collect his handmade shirts from CYC. Susanna didn't hear all that was said, because she was filled with anger and shame. She had allowed herself to be just another of Redfearn's conquests. He didn't need her. He just had to snap his fingers and the nearest female would fall into his arms. All the ecstasy she had known last night dissolved, leaving her only with bitterness and regret.

How easily she'd been taken in by the sad spaniel eyes—he didn't even have to try. She could kick herself. She thought he'd turned to her in love and need. Now she thought about it, there was no word of love spoken. Only the sighed 'Susanna' as he lay, his breath warm on her breasts.

She excused herself then. 'Stay and have some Or Luah here with us. We're going on to the Botanic Gardens,' Matthew begged. But she explained how much shopping she had to do, and that she had to rush to catch Alara in time. She almost ran back to the flat. Then she sent the maid shopping, and retreated to her own room. She was too upset to weep. She lay face upwards on the bed, staring at the fan and wishing she could fade away to nothing, into thin air, taking all her heartache away and allowing some peace of mind to come back. Slowly the tears began to come. Only then did the real extent of her grief become apparent, as the tears turned to storms of sobbing.

It was the right thing to do. When Alara returned, Susanna was composed, quiet, but determined that the one experience must not again trouble her. It was past. It was over. And it meant as little to Susanna as it obviously did to Danny. She helped the maid with the ironing. She rearranged the cutlery in the drawer three times, and watered the trailing ivy by the front door. And by the time Monday morning came round again, Susanna had made herself so physically tired that it was a struggle waking up in the morning.

Never had she been so grateful to have Phil and Jo-Jo at the Pagoda. Always ribbing each other, always so cheerfully content with life, and full of kindness to their patients, they were better than medicine to the lonely Susanna. And with Danny away in Bandar Seri Begawan, she had time to spare to talk to them. 'Where is our beautiful Tilly today, Susanna?' Phil collected his own mail, looking through the pile of opened letters, that had already been neatly put in alphabetical order by a Susanna whose own private life was not allowed to intrude into her efficient dependability.

'Either she's late or she's gone to Brunei with Danny.' Phil twinkled at her. 'And your guess?'

'Well, as you know, I'm not paid to speculate.' Susanna's weekend of tragedy had helped. She now found she could make jokes about the couple.

'Susanna, my dear. You have the best female intuition in the business.'

She nodded. Her new loose hairstyle bounced on her shoulders. She had trimmed the ends, and turned them under this morning. She smiled up at Phil Chan. 'Then I'd be terribly surprised if she isn't in Brunei too.' She leaned on her elbows, and lowered her voice. 'After all, Mr Chan—how on earth will poor Dr Redfearn find his way to the clinic in Bandar Seri Begawan? And he won't know where to find the list of patients, will he?'

'Obviously not.' Phil was grinning, as he turned towards the lift. 'I mean, the poor man only has three postgraduates degrees. That hardly equips him to find his way out of the airport.'

'Morning, Susanna.'

'Hello, Gerry. Nice weekend?'

The tall man looked down, wondering if she was being sarcastic. But she gave him an open smile as she handed him his letters. 'How's your brother?' he asked.

'The flight home is on Wednesday. Thanks for helping him to have the holiday of a lifetime. I believe he's promised to write to the Mettiars' daughters.'

'That is not surprising. But tell him to beware. Pen-friendships can lead to—all sorts of things.' He was laughing with her.

Susanna shook her head. 'At least I know my baby brother now. He's got his head screwed on the right way. I shan't be worrying about Matthew. Just hoping to see him again soon.' Her voice trailed off. It was going to take some time, learning to live alone again.

Mei Li was already in the office, but as Gerry went off to his first patient she came out, holding a square package. 'Sue, I found this by the teapot. It's addressed to you.' She handed over a plain white box. It was sellotaped down, and on the lid was printed 'Sister Susanna Valentine—Administrator'. 'Well, open it, Susanna. I already shook it. If it were a bomb, it would already have gone off.'

'Delivered personally. Maybe it's stationery. But I haven't ordered any recently.' Susanna slit the sticky tape with a slim knife and lifted the lid. Then she carefully drew aside the white tissue paper, which covered a single perfect, deep red rose, with one shiny green leaf, and a fragment of maidenhair fern. There was a narrow satin ribbon round the stem.

'Oh I say . . .' Mei Li gazed with a drooping envy. 'One red rose. That means undying love, you know. Where's the card? Surely it isn't anonymous?'

'There's no card.' Susanna lifted the lovely thing gently, and pulled up the underlying tissue paper. There was a folded paper there. She laid the rose on the desk, while she unwrapped the paper with fingers suddenly unaccountably clumsy.

The letter was very simple. 'I didn't have time to talk before I left. Please let me know how Lucy progresses. If there is any deterioration, I must be told at once. The phone number of this clinic can be got from Mrs Paw. I know you'll do this for me.' There was no signature. But underneath was handwritten 'Thank you Valentine'.

She looked up. Mei Li was staring open-mouthed, waiting for the news. She managed to smile. 'Sorry Mei Li. It isn't undying love at all. It's just our good friend Redfearn getting people to do things for him as per usual.'

'From Danny?'

Susanna handed over the note. 'Sorry your expectations were raised.'

Mei Li read it. 'But it's still lovely to receive flowers.'

'Oh yes.' Susanna showed no more interest in the flower. But Mei Li fetched a small brass Chinese pot, and placed it carefully on the desk.

Susanna spoke to Lucy later. 'Sorry I didn't come at the weekend.'

Lucy Ming was sitting up looking very well. 'My cousin and nephew came. It was nice. They will take me home to their place for a couple of weeks, and when I go back home, they have a young neighbour who has offered to stay with me at nights for another few weeks.'

'I'm glad.' She was making such good progress that Susanna thought the intracranial tumour would soon become a distant memory. Her memory in fact was almost back to normal. She was already looking forward to teaching again after the August holidays. 'Now, I know Dr Nye sees you every day, but will you also let me know if you have any problems at all?'

Lucy Ming smiled broadly. 'I have already been so lucky. To have such a good surgeon as Dr Redfearn, and then to have you so caring for me. I hope I will make no further trouble for you both.'

'It was no trouble. It is wonderful to hear you reminisce—your memory is almost perfect.'

'Yes. Lying here I have gone over my friendship with the Bridget Smith you mentioned. Is there anything else I should remember?'

Susanna shook her head. 'I mustn't prompt you, Lucy.' It didn't matter now. Bridget was at peace—and Bas was who knows where? He could take care of himself, and probably would. He could be in San Francisco by now. He always spoke of the restaurants where he had done the washing up there, as the best he had ever seen.

'Dr Redfearn is consulting at another hospital?'

'Yes. He's in Brunei for a week or two.'

'Alone, Susanna?'

Susanna hesitated. One did not gossip about the staff. 'Er—one of the administrative staff went along too. I think there are papers to sort out.'

Matt's flight was early on Wednesday. Mei Li was to take over Susanna's desk, though it was clear she would have liked to go along too. 'Tell my honorary *tai koh*—you know what that is, Sue?'

'Little brother.'

'Tell *tai koh* good journey. And give him this.' She put a small envelope into Susanna's hand. She smiled. 'Don't worry. It's only a good luck card.'

'My guess is that you'll figure quite prominently in Matt's memories of Singapore.'

'Don't read anything else into it, will you?'

'No. Edinburgh is a long way from here.'

Mei Li added firmly, 'And he has to think of his studies. The next five years are for preparing for his future, not for anything else.'

Susanna smiled, and turned over the envelope in her hand. 'Matt seemed to think that student days were for sowing wild oats. But I daresay he'll soon find out for himself. At least I know he's a good man.' She paused. She sighed. And then she tried to stifle her sigh, but Mei Li had already noticed it. 'I'll be back as soon as the plane takes off.'

'Take your time, Sue. You know Wednesdays are quiet.'

'I'll be back. Don't try to get rid of me.'

'Susanna! I'm not Tilly, you know.'

The roar of jet engines was loud in Changi Airport Lounge. Lush and beautiful surroundings, the fountain, the sculpture—after check-in, Susanna said goodbye to her brother. 'I love you, Sis.'

'I'll be thinking of you. God bless you, Matt.'

A multi-coloured stream of humanity edged towards the passport check at Gate Twelve. Matt turned to join it. Suddenly there was a shout. 'Hey! Matt! Wait, Matt —wait for me.'

Susanna turned sharply. Matthew stopped and put down the bag he was lifting. 'Bas! Hey—nice one, mate.' The lad was running, weaving like a hare between hazards, leaving passengers reeling as he leapt over their trolleys and darted between embracing friends. 'Thanks for coming, Bas.' He grabbed the boy's outstretched hands.

Panting, but smiling, Bas said, 'I had to come. All the best, man.' He puffed a bit more. 'I haven't time to tell you where I'll be. And I'm not sure yet anyway. So—if you don't mind, Susanna—write to me care of Sue. Okay?'

'Sure. I'll do that. You'll hear from me.'

The stream of humanity became inexorable, and Matt was swallowed up into its increasingly urgent flow. One more wave, and Matt had vanished into a bright-looking cavern marked Passport Control. Susanna stood, mesmerised by the crowds, and not wanting to turn away, in case she saw Matt again.

Bas pulled at her sleeve. 'Sue? We could go up. Observation Lounge. Watch the take-off.'

She looked at him. Untidy hair, curling round his tanned lean face, and a pair of sincere blue eyes—with just a hint of green . . . 'Come on then. Where do we go?'

'This way. Just follow me.'

The great Boeings were lined up. Their bulk reduced to toy-size by the distance, each with its own distinctive livery. Matt was taking Singapore Airlines, but they saw Qantas, Thai and Pakistan planes alongside the special blue of the Singapore bird, its three tail feathers perked up and ready to go. 'There they go. The passengers. Matt was near the end.' They stood together for half an hour, while the passengers boarded. The great plane stood patiently, its light flashing. And then it slid easily out of the line, backed on to the runway, and taxied along towards its take-off point. Susanna stared as its huge bulk took to the air like a sparrow. Her brother was being carried across the continents, back to London, back to Mum and Dad. She took out her handkerchief to wave to a speck at a window that she knew was Matthew. Then she hastily used it on her eyes, before looking again at the boy at her side. She wanted to keep him near her. But she knew she had no right.

'Don't cry, Sue. He's going back to five years that will bring him a great life.'

'I know.'

Bas whispered, 'Then stop snivelling, woman.'

She stopped snivelling. 'Bas, I hope you're not going to disappear again. I was very disappointed in you.'

They were walking back now, towards the main exit. The boy said, a trifle sullenly, 'I hope you're not going to lecture me.'

She saw again the frightened deer, the creature that wanted to be friendly but was scared of the implications, of captivity. And she understood. 'No. I promise.'

He tried to explain. 'It isn't that I don't—care— exactly. I just—well—'

'Forget it, Bas.'

They walked in silence. But her tender heart was troubled. She would have loved to show more feelings, but it was not the right time, nor the right technique. 'I'm sure Dad is a decent sort. You like him, don't you, Sue?'

'Yes.' She bit back any further comment. But when he said no more she knew he was waiting for her to tell him more. Did he want to be pleaded with? She didn't know. But it took all her courage then to say, 'There is nobody in the Pagoda I trust more, or admire more.'

'But you don't know the way he treated his family.'

'I have his version.'

'And you believe it more than mine?'

She took a deep breath. 'I've already said I trust him.' They had reached the exit. She turned to Bas. 'You're at Ma Ming's, are you?'

'You'll tell Dad.'

'Forget it then.'

They stood in the sunshine. There was the roar of traffic in the road ahead, and the whine of planes behind them. He said, 'You're going to be a bit lonely without Matt.'

'Yes. For a while, I suppose.'

'I could pop in. Keep you in touch with the beat generation?'

She turned to him and smiled. 'I'd like that.' Then she added, 'Your Dad might be there.'

'So you reckon he's a good sort?'

'Not bad. But I'm not asking you to like him. Only to find out for yourself.'

'Can I be honest with you, Sue?' His pseudo-transatlantic accent had gone now, and she turned to him, hiding her compassion. 'Can I tell you how I really feel?'

She said quietly, as a great jet soared in take-off above them, 'That's the only way between friends.'

'Okay. Then I'll come to you first if my feelings

change. But at the moment—please don't hassle me? You see—it just isn't needed—a father I mean.'

'It's a deal. Maybe not easy. But it's a deal.'

'Hey, Sue—you're not in love with him, are you? It isn't that bad?'

She didn't answer. After a few moments, the boy reached out, and touched her elbow in farewell. 'See you.' And when she turned, he had gone. The airport wasn't too far from where Ma Ming lived. He would probably find his way on foot. Susanna waved for a cab.

Susanna went back to work. Tilly wasn't there. Three days now. There was no doubt at all that she had gone to Brunei with Danny. It was rather underhand, wasn't it, not to have told them in advance? But then again, Susanna was now used to working with the boss's daughter. And though she was a good worker when she chose, her forte was not thinking of other people's feelings. Or their convenience. Tilly did what Tilly wanted, and good luck to her. She might just find Caroline waiting when they got back. Susanna smiled to herself. She might even find herself feeling sorry for Tilly Paw . . .

By Friday, Tilly had found the decency to send them a postcard. It was a view of the coast, with palm trees and high-prowed fishing boats. It read, 'While Dr Redfearn heals the sick, I am making myself useful with the appalling filing system. We were both desperately needed!' But there was no mention of when they were coming back.

The sun was behind the Gold Hill Tower. Susanna sat in the lazy warmth, adding her figures, and entering them neatly. Life seemed to have settled down. Though not yet peaceful, the memory of the Danny she had known that one night, the time when he needed her, began to be precious. He had not been a brute. That night he was as sincere as at any time in his life. She stopped hating what he'd done, what she'd done, and a new maturity crept into her mind. She had her position here, the respect of her doctors, the beauty of the city and a comfortable home. She had Alara to help her, and she had just had her brother to cheer her. How could she possibly complain at such a life?

'I'm through early, Sue.'

'So you are, Gerry.' She took his white coat from him. 'Lucky old you.'

'I'm shattered. Come and have a drink with me.'

She looked at him in surprise. She thought he'd written her off. 'Me?'

'You are Susanna Valentine, aren't you?'

'I think so.'

'So?'

She smiled. He was good-looking. She was lonely. They would both have a happier evening together than apart. 'Nice idea, Gerry.'

'Good.' And he bent over the desk, and kissed her cheek lightly. She didn't mind. Why should she?

CHAPTER NINE

GERRY'S Friday lethargy had miraculously vanished. 'Where do you want to go?'

'Hang on. You may be finished, but I've still got to talk to Mrs Paw, call in at the Hospital to see Lucy, change my clothes, and then . . .'

'Hey, wait.' He sat on the corner of the desk. 'How about me going home and getting a shower. I'll call for you in a couple of hours, and we'll make a night of it?'

She looked down at her fingernails to hide her sudden regret. A night, did he say? That wasn't what she had imagined. Yet he was suddenly full of boyish enthusiasm. She could hardly back out now. 'Right. An evening anyway.'

He took her point, and smiled, his lovely white film-star smile. 'You haven't said where we're going.' The smile reminded her of his glamorous sister.

She took a deep breath. 'Oh—somewhere lavish. Somewhere daring. I'll have to rely on you, because I've never been anywhere like that before.'

'The Palace of Heavenly Delights?'

She burst out laughing. 'Is there really somewhere like that?'

'Of course there is. You might find it a little—well, fast—' But there was fun, not lust in his lively black eyes, and Susanna was ready for her spirits to be lifted. 'I'll be ready.'

He was still sitting on the desk. Now he lifted the single red rose in its little brass container. 'I see you have another admirer, Sue.'

Susanna's smile faded. She picked up the phone. 'I'll

have to get hold of Mrs Paw. It isn't like her to forget to phone.'

'Hmm. I can take a hint. None of your business, Sovani Sahib.' But he smiled good-naturedly, and went off into the Singapore sunset with his usual stylish, leisurely walk.

Dr Roy was following closely on his heels. He was the quietest of her doctors, but always agreeable and appreciative when she did anything for him. He paused at the desk. She hadn't pressed Mrs Paw's private number yet, so Susanna put the phone down again. 'Yes, Dr Roy. Everything okay?'

'Susanna—may I just see the appointment book, to make sure it tallies with mine?' He had taken a small notebook from his pocket. 'Yes, it does. Only revisits.'

'Thank you.' She took the book back from him. 'Is it important?'

He smiled. 'Very. My wife is expecting our second baby in the next few days.'

'How marvellous. Why didn't you tell us?'

'I didn't tell you before, but naturally, I'd like everyone to know now. You see where I have made sure there is a phone number beside each patient? If I am called to my wife, none of these appointments is serious, and they can all be re-scheduled for the following week.'

'Very good.' Susanna made a note. 'And if anyone wants an urgent appointment?'

'Use your discretion. If it sounds vital, then by all means suggest they see Dr Carlton. Otherwise, take the name and phone number, and I'll contact them.' He smoothed back his shiny black hair, not bothering to hide his pleasure. He confided, 'Malika is seven. We were beginning to think she would never have a baby brother.' He nodded. 'Yes, we know it is a boy. The astrologer told us. And she had a scan as well,' he added with a grin. 'You must come to the celebrations as soon as Anni is better.'

She watched him go, his normally precise step rather more hurried than usual. Then she took his white coat to the office, where Mei Li was ready to leave also. 'Coming, Sue?'

'I still haven't heard from Mrs Paw. You go on. I've not visited Lucy yet.'

'Right. Have a lovely peaceful weekend.'

Susanna smiled. The Palace of Heavenly Delights didn't sound awfully peaceful. But she wouldn't say anything until she'd sampled it for herself. She returned to the desk, where she replaced the rose in its former position, before tapping out the digits of her employer's number. 'Mrs Paw? Susanna here.'

'Susanna? I thought you were in Bandar Seri Begawan! I was leaving the accounts till you came back next Friday. What happened?'

'Nothing. Dr Redfearn went to Brunei. And Tilly hasn't been in . . .'

'So Tilly went without you? She must have decided she could manage by herself. Oh well, she knows what she's doing. Give me the figures, dear.'

As Susanna crossed the Japanese garden, she wondered why Tilly hadn't taken her to Brunei. Did she want Danny all to herself? Or was it purely a business arrangement—Tilly could manage the books by herself? Privately Susanna was convinced it was the former. Tilly must have decided to dispense with any competition —especially after meeting Caroline Moore, knowing that she had a prior claim on the handsome surgeon.

Lucy Ming was sitting up writing a letter. She had a gaily coloured bandeau round her naked head, and her face was cheerfully animated. 'Say Lun is coming to take me to Ma's after supper tomorrow. But we'll call in at my place first. Susanna, it is so wonderful to be well again

—to be able to think clearly and remember things.'

'Come and see me when you're quite well.'

'I hope you'll come to Ma's.' The woman smiled, and held out a folded paper. 'After the trouble you went to to find her for me, I've drawn a map—how to reach her place from the bus station.'

Susanna took it with a rueful smile as she recalled her sticky and unfruitful search for Ma Ming. 'And perhaps Bas will be around? Did Say Lun mention him?'

'Oh yes, lah. He does stay there sometimes. And he is talking of attending the local technical college . . .' She broke off in amazement, as her sedate visitor jumped up from her chair and cheered. 'What are you doing?'

'Sorry, Lucy. Bas at college? I can't believe it. It must be my birthday.' And she went home to change in a glow of optimism. If only it came true, and Bas settled down after everything. Perhaps even if he didn't actually go back to Danny—he might at least be influenced slightly by his father's standing in the community to try and better himself.

So, what did a lady wear to be escorted to the Palace of Heavenly Delights? She decided on her best silk cheongsam, which was the colour of cinnamon, decorated with pearls round the neck and the slit sides, and showed off her hair colour very well. She wore pearl drops in her ears, and sandals in pearlised leather. She stood for a moment before the mirror. Did she recognise the woman who stared rather brazenly back at her? She shook the mane of pale hair and didn't care. Tonight she would see what delights were left to her, as the regiment of women with claws in Danny Redfearn was too powerful for her to try to beat. And too powerful for him too. Susanna couldn't see Danny sending both Tilly and Caroline packing. He was too easy-going.

A low hoot from a car-horn outside meant Gerry was waiting. With a final toss of her head, she closed the

front door behind her and ran downstairs. She was lucky
to have a man such as Gerry Sovani tonight—so strong,
so coolly lustful, so fiercely masculine . . . He leaned
over to open the door for her, and kissed her cheek
lingeringly. She saw his eyes narrow in approval as he
surveyed her from head to toe—and then spent rather
more time surveying the bit in between. He started the
Mercedes, and they slid out into the evening bustle of
traffic. 'Still the Palace of Heavenly Delights?'

Susanna grinned. It sounded so ridiculous. 'Why not?'

'It might live up to its name.'

Susanna looked down at her painted fingernails. 'I
don't believe that for a minute. I'm coming out of
curiosity, that's all.'

Slightly disappointed, Gerry was nevertheless a
textbook escort. He played smoochy songs on his
quadrophonic player before they arrived at a small
entrance in the city centre which Susanna had never
even noticed in the daytime. The archway was outlined
in neon. The name was around it in English and in
Chinese, and just inside the glittering entrance stood
two Chinese girls dressed in white, with tinsel wings, and
two men dressed in black catsuits. Susanna tried not to
stare as Gerry showed his membership card. He bent
and whispered in her ear, 'They're the bouncers.'

'What? The girls as well?'

'Oh yes. Those girls are kung fu experts. I've seen
them in action.'

Susanna said innocently, 'Then we must remember
not to get too rowdy, Gerry.'

They entered down a steep staircase. Gerry said, 'I'm
not sure that I know you in this mood, but I'm dying to
find out.' He had swiftly ushered her to a table in the
dimly lit room, where a waiter bowed deeply and
brought a shining pail with a green bottle covered with
condensation before they had time to settle themselves

at the table. In reply to Susanna's amused look, he said,
'Yes—I do come here often. And yes, I always drink the
same brand of champagne.'

Susanna twisted the bottle to see the label. But the
waiter sprang to help her at once, and showed it her
before opening the bottle with a skilful twist of his
thumbs, and a dextrous move with the tall glass to catch
the subsequent foaming liquid before any of it spilled.
'Dom Perignon—1976. Mmm, that is a good year,' she
joked.

'Of course it is.' Gerry didn't realise she was joking
out of complete ignorance. 'Apart from dowdy women,
one of my pet hates is cheap champagne.'

Susanna didn't reply, instead looking around in the
dark, to see the kind of people who frequented the
Palace of Heavenly Peace, and who could afford the best
champagne. It was hard to diagnose, except that there
must have been a lot of wealthy Chinese businessmen.
Some were grossly fat, but many of them had clearly
gone in for the latest health craze, and looked fit and slim
as their doll-like women.

She was aroused by the clink of his glass on hers.
'Sorry. Cheers.'

'Well, what do you think?'

'Wow.' She looked around again, and said, 'I don't
think I really fit in here.'

'Well, you did say you wanted a daring evening.'

'I did?'

'Don't joke. And don't act like a tiresome little
virgin.'

Susanna felt her face colour. Fortunately the lighting
was far too dim for it to matter. She said, feeling the
novelty suddenly wear a bit thin, 'I haven't ever been to
this sort of place. And I don't usually drink champagne.
You did know that before we came.'

'Yes, honey, I'm sorry.' He lifted his glass towards

her. 'But you are a lovely woman. Here's to happiness. I hope you find it.'

'You're cynical, Gerry.'

'Possibly. Happiness is an overrated word.'

She was silent for a moment. The thumping rhythm of the beat music from the tinsel-spangled band in an alcove enveloped them in sound. It was good, in a way. It took away the need to think—even the ability to do so. She sipped the champagne, beginning to enjoy it. It was very fizzy, and the sensation was exhilarating. She allowed it to sparkle over her nose before drinking again—and then had to have her nose dried by Gerry's handkerchief. They were both laughing when he said quietly, 'Are you going to come home with me tonight?'

The atmosphere, the champagne and the deep look in his beautiful eyes combined to make a certain magic. 'I don't know.'

'It could be Paradise.'

'I believe you. But for how long?'

She expected him to be annoyed, but he leaned back and turned off the seduction button for a moment. 'Good question. Not very long, I suppose.' He drank from his glass, and the waiter materialised to refill them both. Then he said with a wrinkled forehead, 'You know, Sue, you are beginning to sound like my mother.'

'Indrani said that your mother liked me.'

'She did. Why aren't you a Brahmin, Susanna? Then we could live happily ever after.'

'Gerry, you know we couldn't. Don't you remember telling me the way it ought to be between two people? There has to be something special, or it won't work out. You said it. Your own words.'

'Yes I know.' He smiled then, and his face was sincere. 'But I like being with you. You are quite fun, and terribly pretty. Wouldn't that see us through?'

'I doubt it. I think we'd be finished after the first

blazing row.' She was speaking with a bantering tone, but she began to see that Gerry was more than half serious. Quickly she said, 'So cross me off your list, and dance with me. Show me how to do that.' And she pointed discreetly to a couple on the floor who were dancing seductively together, yet without actually touching at all.

'That takes years of practice,' he said. 'And it's a courtship ritual. It arouses the senses to such a pitch that—well—the next step is inevitable—bed.'

Susanna looked down now. The sparkle had flattened, and she felt threatened. She was in the wrong place, and she wanted to get out. The thought of her lovemaking with Danny was tarnished suddenly—this place gave her memory an uncomfortable feeling of being made public and cheapened. Then Gerry was behind her, holding her chair. 'Sorry again. Come on, let's dance nice and sedately. Just hold me close and listen to the music, okay?'

'Okay.' But she couldn't bring a smile to her face now. She held Gerry gingerly. He held her firmly in his strong expressive hands. She recalled that night at the Carltons when she had found it thrilling and sensuous. Now it was only a touch and it meant nothing to her. And it made her miss Danny Redfearn terribly.

After a few moments it must have been obvious to Gerry that she was not responding to his physical manipulation. She began to feel that it would be better to give up now rather than go on hoping to bring the evening to life again.

'Excuse me.'

They stopped dancing and turned to look who had inserted a red-talonned hand between them. Susanna stared. It was Caroline Moore. She was wearing a low-cut blue gown and lot of make-up. And she was quite drunk. 'Caroline!'

'Hi, Susanna. Fancy meeting you here. And Gerry darling—how lovely to see you again.'

'Hello, Caroline. Will you join us?' He led them both to the table, and the waiter swiftly emptied the remaining champagne into three glasses.

Susanna said, 'You two have met?'

Gerry nodded, and she saw his eyes do a quick once-over of Caroline Moore's apparel with apparent interest. 'Yes—at the country club. You are alone, Caroline?'

'All alone, darling. The Carltons wanted to go to the theatre, so I told them I'd amuse myself.' She giggled, and allowed her hand to stray on the table to touch Gerry's. 'So I am. I hope you don't mind me cutting in.'

'Of course not.' Susanna was being quite truthful. 'Why don't you dance with Caroline, Gerry?'

'You would like to?' But the brunette was already attaching herself to Gerry in a barnacle-like grip. Susanna smiled to herself. Caroline could make a fool of herself if she wanted. And she may even have saved Gerry from total boredom. She decided that it would probably be quite in order for her to slip out and take a taxi home—in fact, it was the ideal solution. She picked up her purse, and went across the dim floor towards the Powder Room.

There was a scream. The music was so loud that few people noticed it. But a man had slumped to the floor, toppling his chair just by Susanna's foot. She stepped back, and then knelt at once by the stricken person. His face was convulsed with pain, and his breath was coming in gasps. She had seen it before. Cardiac arrest. But here was no resuscitation trolley. 'Get an ambulance.' She didn't waste time arguing with the others at the table, but bent at once to listen to the prostrate man's chest. She could hear nothing. Desperately she began external cardiac massage, thrusting her closed fists over his sternum with as much strength as she could muster. Every few thumps, she bent her head to try to detect any signs of life. It seemed like a week. Thump, thump. Her hands ached. She heard Gerry's voice behind her. 'Keep going, Sue!' And she was dimly aware of his blue-black head close to hers, as he forced open the victim's mouth and tried to direct life-giving air to the closed lungs.

They were in a small circle, where emergency lights had been brought, although lights made no difference to her desperate failing attempts to start the arrested heart. 'Beat, damn you, beat!' It was her voice, although she didn't recall saying anything. Only thinking it—praying it . . .

'Ambulance is here!'

'It's all right. I'm a doctor.' He was only a child. Tousled hair and horn-rimmed glasses, but he had felt the patient's pulse, and had heard something. 'I'll take over. Get the stretcher. He's going to be all right.'

'I'll go with him.' The horn-rimmed child. Susanna stood back. The pageant before her gradually vanished, and the music started again.

'Come and sit down.'

Susanna sat down, but suddenly she couldn't keep awake. 'Get me a cab, Gerry.'

'We'll take you.'

Dreamlike, she was led out to the Mercedes she recognised. Caroline was there. Gerry took her up to her flat, opened the door for her. He led her in. 'Are you all right?'

'Yes, Good night.'

He waited until he was sure. Then he went back to the Mercedes, and the awaiting Caroline . . .

Susanna ran to her bed, and lay down, taking off her clothes, and resting naked on the coverlet. A life. She had saved a life . . . And at the same time, from far off

inside her head came a tremendous sense of relief. She
had saved herself too.

Next day she went over to Changi. Lucy's map was good
and this time Susanna did not get lost. The secret had
been a flight of steps, quite near the bus station, that led
her to a totally different area from the one where she
searched the last time. The lighted basement was clear
and welcoming. She went into the back room, where
Lucy was lying like Cleopatra on the comfortable
sofa. Ma was there, and Say Lun. They sat together
for a while, drinking tea, and talking over the good
luck that had cured Lucy of her tumour in time to save
her life.

Susanna said, 'Bas has been, Ma?'

'Ai-oh, that boy. Sometimes he here, sometimes not.
How I worry.'

'Did you know Bridget Smith, Ma?'

'I know her. She sad lady. Bas good boy, very bright,
very sweet, lah.'

Susanna said carefully, 'You know that Dr Redfearn
is father of Bas? You know why Lucy should go to him?
It seems too much a coincidence.'

'Why?' Ma was practical. 'If Lucy has the pain in the
head, then the doctor tell her who to go to.'

'Who is her doctor?'

'Lee. He live round the corner. But he not like that
you call at night.'

'I daresay. But he won't mind if I tell him it isn't a
housecall.'

She was out of the door when Ma called, 'He bad-
tempered man.'

Susanna stuck her head in. 'I bad-tempered woman,
lah.'

Dr Lee was in, and was having his supper. But
Susanna put on her best official air. 'I'm Sister Valentine

from the Pagoda Hospital. It is important to know why you sent Miss Lucy Ming to Dr Redfearn.'

The doctor frowned. 'Why I sent her? No reason. I told her the names of two or three neurologists that I knew. When I said that a new doctor had arrived at the Pagoda who had written books on the subject, she chose him. That is all.'

'Was her mind clear?'

'Not at all. She seemed in a dream world of her own.'

'But she chose Dr Redfearn. Did you mention the name to her?'

'I did. I knew his name from articles in the *Lancet*. I knew he was good.'

'Did she show any sign at all of knowing his name?'

Dr Lee hesitated before replying. 'Possibly, possibly.'

'Oh, please tell me how?'

He spoke slowly now, forgetting his supper. 'Well, I reeled off the names I knew at the City Hospital. When I said Redfearn, she interrupted me. She said "I'll see him" immediately, without waiting for any other names.'

Susanna felt like a lawyer as she said, 'Dr Lee—did you think she made that choice just because the name happened to be familiar to her?'

'It is very possible. Very possible.'

'But she didn't say she knew it?'

'No. And she still doesn't know it, young lady. I was there when she came home, and she had no knowledge of the name.'

Susanna retraced her steps to the café. Lucy was looking tired, so she didn't stay longer. 'See you all soon.' And she turned towards the street.

It was a mystery. Lucy seemed to have known the Redfearn name. Yet it meant nothing to her now, even though her memory had returned almost completely.

It was quite a walk from the bus station in town.

Susanna could have taken a cab or a trishaw, but she wanted to walk. She wanted to think over all she had been through. Life had erupted when Danny Redfearn had arrived at the Pagoda. Things were happening to her that she had never envisaged—like falling for a man who could never love her in the same way. Like finding a boy who needed his father, and yet refused to go to him. And like meeting a schoolteacher who seemed to hold some secret—and yet could remember none. 'Oh Danny, help me.' The words were in her mind, not aloud.

And then she came to the temple near her flat. The evening crowds were passing the lion doors. Some entered and lit a stick of incense, but most passed without a second glance. Susanna stopped. She went in the open doors, but stopped just inside. She felt as though she were trespassing. She slipped her shoes off.

One of the worshippers who passed her on the way out stopped and looked at her. It was a tiny woman, fifty or sixty years old. On her lined face was a sweet expression of calm and benevolence. 'You are English?'

Susanna nodded. She was Singaporean, but English would do as opposed to Chinese. The little woman picked up a stick of incense, and pointed to the golden altar. 'There. Speak your prayer. God always hears.'

'Thank you.'

'You do not believe, do you?'

'My problems are a bit complicated.' Susanna smiled at the kindness of a total stranger.

'Go. You will see. They can be combed free by the spirit. Free as silk. Smooth as your own hair, child. Go now.'

Touched by her words, Susanna approached the altar, and lit the incense at the flickering flame. Now—what did she want? For Lucy, for Bas, for Danny—or for herself? She bent her head, she must say something or else why was she here? And then some words came. And she said inside herself, 'You know all. Please help.'

No miracle happened. No flash of lightning, or the sudden inspiration to know what was best to do. But having said the words, her mind was eased. She bent her head once more, and left the temple, picking up her sandals at the door.

She turned the key in her lock, and entered, feeling terribly tired. Even the thought that Danny Redfearn would have returned from Brunei by now did not stimulate her, knowing that he was too busy a man to have time to call and visit his receptionist and theatre sister. She took off her sandals for the second time within the half hour, and walked slowly into the lounge. Then she saw a light in the kitchen. Surely she had not left that on? It had been broad daylight when she had her morning coffee in there.

Then a voice came from the kitchen. 'Is that you, Sue? Want some cocoa?'

'Hello, Bas.' She was suddenly delighted that he had come back to her.

CHAPTER TEN

THE boy sat on the floor at Susanna's feet. They drank cocoa in silence, listening to the Sunday night traffic and the crickets singing their inevitable shrill accompaniment. After a while Bas said, 'You don't mind me coming like this? It does seem a bit cheeky of me just to walk in.'

'I don't mind, really.' She looked down at the curly untidy head.

'I did bring my own cocoa.'

'Oh Bas.' How did she tell the boy that she was glad he trusted her. Of course he had Ma Ming, but he didn't have a real home, and that hurt her soft heart. She couldn't have turned him away even if he didn't belong to Danny. The fact that he was Danny's flesh and blood made him more special, of course.

'Seen Dad lately?' He was being rather sarcastic, using the name in a mocking way. But she didn't mind that—at least he was interested.

'He's been to the Bandar Seri Begawan Hospital. I believe he was coming home today.' She didn't say that she'd been hoping he might have been in touch with her—if only to enquire about Lucy.

'You sound a bit sad. Why don't you give him a ring—see if he's back?' He looked up from under the mop of hair, and he wasn't joking with her. 'Go on. I can tell you're thinking about him.'

She met his clear gaze. Yes, he was perceptive all right. Sensitive—like his father. She couldn't help smiling. 'I didn't say you could stay at my house if you're going to bully me. I don't bully *you*, do I?'

143

He agreed. 'Okay. But—see if he's in anyway. It's no skin off your nose, is it?' He finished his cocoa, and took the mugs to the kitchen. When he came back he was carrying his precious guitar. He squatted on the sofa and played a couple of chords. 'Mind if I play?'

'Not a bit. But keep it cool. I don't like to disturb the neighbours this late.'

Bas started to play. He didn't know any elaborate melodies, but the tunes he picked out were neatly played. He seemed to forget that she was there, playing only for himself—softly and with feeling. Then he sang:

> 'Are you going to Scarborough Fair?
> Parsley, sage, rosemary and thyme,
> Remember me to one who lives there,
> She was once a true love of mine.'

Susanna said nothing, but she reached out and dialled the number of Danny's flat. She couldn't go to bed without hearing if he was back or not.

The phone rang in Danny's room. One, twice, three times—

'Yes? Hello?'

A woman's voice. Susanna hated herself for ringing. 'Caroline? It's Susanna here. I just wondered how Danny got on in Brunei.' She tried not to falter as she spoke, sensing across the line that the woman was most annoyed to hear her.

'Well, it's a bit late, Susanna. He's in the shower. I'll get him to phone you back.'

'It doesn't matter.' She put the phone down. Bas had stopped playing. 'I'd better go to bed. Work in the morning,' she said to him.

'Can I have the sofa?'

'You can have the spare room. You know that.'

She didn't sleep for a long time, wondering if Danny would ring—if Caroline would even give him the message. But all was quiet, and she drifted to sleep eventually. She dreamed sad dreams—about being on a lonely sea-shore. The one boat that appeared out of the mist didn't seem to spot her, and drifted off again out of sight . . .

She was awakened by the telephone, and shot to answer it. 'Yes? Susanna Valentine?'

'Ellen Paw here, dear. Did I wake you?'

'Not at all,' she lied. 'I'm almost ready.'

'Good. Well, two things that couldn't wait, Susanna. First is congratulations.'

'What for?'

'Don't joke, Susanna. You're a heroine, lah. You are the one who saved the life of the gentleman in the nightclub, aren't you?'

'Oh—that. Yes, I did give him cardiac massage. But it's nothing special. I am a nurse, and I knew what to do—so I did it.'

'Nothing special maybe. But you've heard of Heng Sing Enterprises?'

'Yes. A huge multi-national thing. Everyone has heard of it.'

'Well—that was Mr Heng.'

'Honestly?'

'Honestly. He's a friend of ours.'

'How is he?'

'Very well—and singing your praises. He wants to see you, but I had to tell him that I'm asking you to fly to Brunei this morning for a week.'

'Brunei? Me?'

'Yes. Tilly hasn't finished the work there. Do you mind? Can you go at short notice?'

'Naturally I can. Mei Li deputises for me at the desk, and Sister Silvano or Sister Greig can do Theatre for me.'

'Well, I'll arrange for them to be told. Be at the airport

for ten. There's a ticket waiting for you at the MAS desk.
And Dr Nanda will make sure someone is at Bandar Seri
Begawan to meet you. Pack for one week.'

'Very well, Mrs Paw.'

'Thank you, dear.'

Susanna drank some coffee. Packing and going to
Brunei was no problem, but she realised that it would
have been better if she'd gone with Tilly in the first place.
Between them they would have finished the paper-work.
As it was, it appeared very much as though Tilly had
spent the time with Danny Redfearn instead of getting
on with the filing. And now it would be yet another week
before she saw Danny again. Oh well. Maybe the en-
forced separation would help her get over her infatua-
tion for the man. Maybe.

She walked downstairs with her flight bag. Bas was
still asleep, and she didn't wake him. There was no need
to tell him what was going on. He could come and go
without telling her, and she could do the same. She knew
she could trust Bas. Alara might be a bit surprised, but
she was a phlegmatic lady, who would take it in her
stride.

Susanna intended looking for a cab, but as she came
out of the apartment entrance, she saw a smiling Ahmad
with the Pagoda limousine. 'I have to take you to
Changi, Miss Valentine.'

'That's good. I didn't fancy taking a cab during rush
hour.' Rush hour was just beginning, as the gentle mist
lifted from the beautiful vibrant face of the city. Susanna
settled back to enjoy the comfort of the Mercedes. The
dew was still on the palm leaves, and the great hanging
banana leaves on the roadside trees. The smell of petrol
and diesel hadn't had time to overcome the fragrance of
the flowers and new grass.

And so Susanna was back at the airport so soon after
seeing Matthew off. She reflected on that day—on the

way Bas had scurried up like a terrier—not wanting to be seen, and yet unwilling to let his friend go without wishing him well.

This morning she was the traveller. She climbed up the metal steps into the Airbus along with business people of all sizes and shapes. She saw the Jumbos, like grounded birds patiently waiting for their great bulk to be coaxed into motion. She settled herself in a seat with a fashion magazine. It was almost like a holiday. She tipped the seat back a little.

There was just one small niggle of doubt. Her reasons for Tilly not completing the work were no doubt true. Tilly wouldn't have slaved over a hot filing system if Danny Redfearn had finished his clinic. But another idea had come to Susanna—not immediately, for her own mind was not as devious as Tilly's. It was that Tilly might make use of her absence to take over Susanna's job. The thought of that pert and pretty little figure presiding in the foyer irritated her. She slammed the magazine on the little table in front of her—and then apoligised to the man in the next seat.

'Please do not worry. I have done my morning meditation. Nothing will intrude into my serenity today.' He was a perfectly ordinary businessman with spectacles and a briefcase. Susanna looked at him curiously. His face was smooth and unruffled. He saw her stare. 'You look surprised.'

She turned away with a slight blush. 'Not surprised. Envious. It must be marvellous to have complete control. Not to let small things worry you.' A thought struck her. 'What about big things?'

'It depends what you mean by big things. A clear mind helps me to concentrate on important deals.'

'I see. But what about—well—emotional problems?'

His face was perfectly stolid. 'I have none.'

The plane was ready for take-off, and they fastened

their seat belts obediently. But Susanna was still in a
questioning mood. 'Then your response to beautiful
things must be dulled surely? Lovely flowers, beautiful
music?'

'Enhanced.'

She didn't go on, but she thought a lot during the short
flight across to Brunei. That chap had got hold of something that sounded pretty useful. She could do with a
dose of meditation. She would try it as soon as she had a
spare moment. There were bound to be spare moments
in Brunei, seeing that she knew nobody at all.

The rain was pouring steadily when they disembarked. Susanna ran for cover. It was very hot and
humid in the airport, and the rain drummed on the roof
with an unwelcoming monotony. Irritated and annoyed
to find there was no one there to meet her, she thought
again of her Buddhist travelling companion, and wished
she'd asked him a bit more about instant meditation.

'Miss Valentine?'

An elderly Bentley stood outside, driven by a good-
natured young lad with an inordinate pride in his job. In
spite of the heat he wore a peaked chauffeur's cap, and
he insisted on being allowed to open and close the doors
for her. And after feeling the hinges grate a little rustily,
Susanna was happy to let him. She didn't want to add
to her troubles by making a door drop off the official
car.

She saw little of the town that looked outstanding
through the rain. They were soon driving through fields
with sad-looking bullocks standing patiently dripping
wet. Then they came to a low single-storey building with
a green roof, and low eaves pouring into the gutters
below.

'Nice place, lah?' The lad ushed her inside quickly,
and went back for her bag. 'I show you Dr Nanda.'

The main office was off the front hall, and Dr Nanda

was seated within. He looked up, a gruff elderly gentleman with a starched collar and impeccable tie in spite of
the overwhelming heat. His hair was luxuriant and pure
white. His gruffness faded when he saw Susanna. 'Come
in, come in. So pleased to meet you.' He apologised for
the state of the office. 'I ought to have had this place
organised better, but I've been so busy with patients.
Our turnover has increased rapidly—more than I could
cope with I am afraid.'

'Miss Paw has started getting records in order?'

'Yes. Very efficient lady, but there is still a lot to do.
Oh—mind the paint.' There was a pile of new paint tins
in the corridor, as he took her out to show her to her
quarters. 'She insisted that we decorate everything. The
painters will be starting today.'

The records office was in rather a mess, though
Susanna soon saw that more than half the record cards
were now in alphabetical order. That wasn't a bad start.
'Do you think the painters could start in here, please?
It's no use putting everything away if it has to be taken
out when they start.'

'Absolutely right. Well done, Miss Valentine. I'll see
to it when they arrive.'

'I'll take over in the office, if you like, Doctor. You
must have patients to see?'

'Yes, yes, I do. Thank you, thank you.' He left her to
unpack in a small back room overlooking the dripping
garden. Trees outside her window hung their great
fronds in a damp greeting. She smiled grimly to herself.
Not much of a holiday after all.

She knew where the staff lounge was. After changing,
she went along where she was told she only had to press a
bell and a maid would bring her coffee. She entered the
room—somehow deserted, as though all the occupants
had vanished like the crew of the *Marie Celeste*. Then
she smiled at an old upright piano in one corner. She

pressed the bell on the wall, and went over to see if there was any music in the battered piano stool.

But there was something already on the stand. She picked it up. It was by Debussy. And the title stood out, because it wasn't in French but in English. 'The Girl with Flaxen Hair.'

She sat down, suddenly very weak. So many images flashed into her mind at that name. She saw Danny on that first night party, standing against a palm tree trunk, describing his own imaginary flaxen-haired girl . . . She remembered when he had touched her hair with hands as light as a butterfly, as they stood together in the sun-dappled Japanese garden . . . and she thought of him lying in her arms, murmuring 'Susanna' as though it were a prayer.

'I'm sorry.' She hadn't seen the little Malay maid. 'Coffee, please.'

The maid was chatty. 'You play piano? Doctor play very good.'

'Dr Nanda?'

'No no. New Doctor, come last week. Play very good.'

Susanna showed the piece she had taken from the piano. 'This?'

'I do not know.'

Susanna replaced the music, and sat down, feeling the yellowing keys. She hadn't touched a piano for years. But the notes came back to her, as she played the opening bars lightly, imagining the girl that Danny loved to imagine—light, pretty, natural . . . And suddenly she stopped, seeing Tilly Paw taking that place in his heart. And she banged the lid down.

'That is the same. You play nice too.'

'Please—can I have some coffee?'

The corridors and rooms began to look better as the painters got to work. The sun shone on the little hospital, and the flowers bloomed. It was quite a pretty place really, and Susanna put in many hours, making sure that the notes were all in order and easy to keep so. She ordered new stationery, and made sure that the suppliers in the town would send a representative every six months.

'I'd like your advice about the office.' It was the last place to have the painters in, and Dr Nanda was standing with the chief painter, both holding colour charts in front of them.

'You are the one who has to live with it, Dr Nanda.'

'Not really, Miss Valentine. I'm retiring at Christmas. I'll only see it for six months. And as I'm told you might be interested in the post, it might be a good idea if you chose. I like that blue myself. It goes with your eyes. And a touch of white. And why not pick out the mouldings round the door and windows with gold? That would be very smart.'

Susanna was silent. It must have been Tilly. Tilly was plotting to send Susanna to work here, and take over the Pagoda job after all. She felt betrayed—and yet Tilly had never been the sort one trusted. She might have expected something like this from her.

She was furious with her. How could she think she could manipulate people like that? Susanna loved her job, her little flat. She loved the noise of the Gold Hill Plaza, and she loved the fragrances of the street hawker stalls, the magnificence of the Temple, the gaiety of the people and the sheer exhilarating vitality of the bustling, seething crowd in the neon-lit evenings. She loved the colours, and the sounds and the smells of Singapore. And to come to a small quiet place like this would be like banishing her from Paradise. She would not do it. She would give up her job first.

Fortunately for Dr Nanda, a nurse appeared at the door. 'It's one of Dr Redfearn's epileptic patients. She has come to the hospital with a red rash, and she thinks it is the tablets Dr Redfearn gave her.'

'I'll come along. Do you want to see her, Miss Valentine?'

'Oh yes please.' They accompanied the nurse back along the now sweet-smelling corridor, the new paint shining in the sun. 'What drugs is this patient on?'

The nurse hesitated. 'Phenytoin I think.'

Dr Nanda looked at Susanna. 'You have seen a reaction to Phenytoin, Miss Valentine?'

'Yes. A long time ago, but the patient was in a lot of pain.'

'It can be bad. Fortunately a change of tablets usually does the trick. Of course you know that only three per cent of people ever have any reaction. It is very rare.'

Dr Nanda was reassuring with the lady, a small Malay with a skin rash. He examined her thoroughly. 'You have taken the tablets regularly?'

'Yes.'

Susanna said, 'Shall I bring her notes? What is your name?'

'I am Mrs Chanaisingam.'

Nanda said, 'No need to go back to the office. I am sure this is not a reaction. It looks very like scarlet fever to me. There's no eyelid swelling.'

Susanna insisted. 'Doctor, the notes will still be in the clinic. The new rules say that they are only filed after three months. They are just here in the drawer. See? Now we can check what Dr Redfearn wrote about this lady.' And she handed the folder to him.

He took it with a tolerant smile, and they looked at the latest page together. There in Danny's neat writing was the comment, 'Showed some sensitivity to Carbamazepine. Phenytoin commenced today 200 mgs t.i.d. Sensitivity will show up in one to three weeks.

If so, suggest immediate change to sodium valproate before symptoms become distressing.'

Dr Nanda nodded. 'Well done.' He wrote the prescription at once, and gave the patient careful instructions to return to be checked up weekly. He smiled at Susanna. 'Now you see how we need you, Miss Valentine.'

She couldn't help smiling at his subterfuge. 'I'll train someone for you, if you like. It isn't me as an individual you need—just someone who cares about being tidy, and likes things done properly.'

She didn't want to work here. And even if she liked the place, the fact that Tilly Paw had almost decided everything for her would have made Susanna refuse it. She was an easy-going person, slow to anger. But being assigned to Bandar Seri Begawan by Tilly Paw was like being posted to Alaska. Especially if she did it to keep Susanna from being yet another woman rival when it came to Danny Redfearn.

However, when it was time to leave, she had to admit that it wasn't the last place in the world. It was peaceful and the countryside was smooth and tranquil when it wasn't raining. There was always mist in the early mornings over the gentle pastures and flat paddy fields, rising like some pale green wood nymphs among the trees that fringed the fields.

Her little chauffeur was waiting. He bowed as she got out at the airport, and she gave him a fifty-dollar bill. 'I've never had such a smart driver.' His eyes widened when he saw the value. And he bowed again, much lower.

There was no composed Buddhist on the flight back, only a rather tipsy salesman who offered Susanna a lift when they disembarked. She was glad to see the Pagoda car waiting for her, and made her escape the moment she had passed Customs.

Ahmad had a message. 'If you agreeable, Dr Roy send his compliments and there is small party for birth of his son.'

'Now?' Susanna looked at her watch. It was five-thirty.

'At seven. I will come for you. All Pagoda doctors going.'

'Naturally. Dr Roy must be delighted. Would it be any trouble to take me round to Orchard Road to buy something for the baby?'

Her apartment was empty. There was no sign that Bas had been there at all, apart from a lowering of the level of cocoa in the jar. She was a bit sorry. It would have been nice to have a welcome from someone who she cared for.

When Ahmad came back for her, she was ready. She wore a simple raw silk blouse in deep red over a skirt of cream. And she carried a silver cup for Dr Roy's new son, and a bouquet of roses for his wife. It was heartening to be back among the atmosphere she loved. And it would be good to meet 'her' doctors again. She had already forgotten the week in Brunei, at the prospect of getting back to normal at the Pagoda again.

The car drew up outside Dr Roy's unpretentious little white house on the outskirts of Jurong. 'Thank you, Ahmad.' She could see through the windows where Mrs Roy stood, dark and attractive in a yellow and silver sari, holding the baby in her arms. Dr Carlton was standing closest, and Susanna could see Fenella Carlton making cooing noises at the child.

And then she saw Danny. He stood alone in a corner, looking with mild interest at a picture on the wall. It was so good to see him. Living with Caroline he may be, too busy to telephone Susanna he obviously was—yet she couldn't hate him. His lean shape, his brown curls, the slightly narrowed green eyes . . . She saw him again as a

cowboy in check shirt and high boots, aloof and somehow not fitting in with the conventionally neat and
prosaic setting. Yet he wore conventional grey trousers,
a white short-sleeved shirt. And his tie was only a little
bit crooked . . . As she waited at the door after ringing
the bell, she knew that just the knowledge that he was
there was making her heart rate increase, and her
breathing irregular.

Then she was among them. Handshakes, congratulations, greetings—there was no chance to collect her
thoughts for a while. Goh Min Chan, Phil's wife, was
holding the baby now, and Susanna went to peep at the
small brown face, the mop of spiky black hair, the
adorable tiny fingers that clutched at hers as she touched
them. She felt a lump in her throat at the complete
perfection in the tiny form. 'God bless you.'

Goh Min smiled. 'Susanna, you are looking broody
now. Your turn to hold him.'

'Oh yes please. Unaccustomed as I am,' she smiled,
taking the small incredibly light bundle. 'But I'm sure
Anni wants him to go to sleep now.' She looked at his
mother's face. Surely she didn't want her precious child
passed around like a living parcel.

Anni laughed. 'Don't worry. He is like his Daddy. He
will fall asleep anywhere.'

Then Gerry was there, holding the child's fingers, and
whispering in Susanna's ear. 'You certainly look sweet
like that.'

'Hello again, Gerry.'

'You heard about Mr Heng?'

'Who?' Susanna allowed the baby to be passed back to
his mother. 'Oh—that Mr Heng. He is all right?'

'He wants to reward us.' He smiled. 'It was a funny
sort of date. You weren't mad at me, were you?'

'Of course not. I was afraid I'd spoiled the evening for
you.'

'It wasn't entirely spoiled.' He winked. And then over his tall shoulders, she saw that Danny Redfearn was staring at her. She couldn't read his eyes, but they weren't twinkling. And they weren't peaceful. She felt a shiver down her spine. As soon as she could, she went over to him.

'It seems a long time since we—we talked.' Not being able to read his face made it difficult to think of the right thing to say.

'Two weeks. Did you enjoy Brunei?'

'Not much.'

'I thought you were going to—' he broke off. 'I must have got it wrong.'

Tilly had told him she was going to work there. Annoyed, Susanna said, 'I'll tell you if I'm changing my plans. At the moment I work at the Pagoda.'

As though unable to stop himself Danny said, 'And go out with Gerry Sovani.' His look was readable now. It said that anyone who goes out with Gerry Sovani is a gold-digging playgirl.

At that moment, Caroline Moore came into the room. Her dress was undone at the neck, and her elaborately waved dark hair was ruffled. She came across to Danny at once, and put her hand through the crook of his elbow. 'Shall we go home, darling?' Her speech was slurred.

Susanna looked at her in horror. Caroline looked drunk. Yet there was only a bottle of medium sherry going the rounds. Susanna looked at Danny. He was watching her closely. For a long moment they seemed incapable of looking away from each other. The sight of that piece of music on the battered old piano in Brunei came into her mind, and the rush of tenderness that came with it. Poor Danny. Life was trampling on his dreams.

And then she looked again at the brunette, from

whose clinging talons he had made no effort to withdraw. Poor Danny nothing! He was in charge of his own life. He didn't have to stick by Caroline. He could go out and look for his flaxen-haired ideal if he wanted to. He was too lazy, that was his trouble. Too idle and too comfortable with the way things were.

Sarcastically she repeated Caroline's words. 'Yes, you'd better go home, darling.' And she didn't look as she went over to talk to Fenella Carlton.

CHAPTER ELEVEN

In spite of her brave words, Susanna was bitterly disappointed. She hadn't expected Danny to fall into her arms, but the least she had expected was a share in his cool easy conversation, his gentle green glances and his smooth distinctive voice. She expected the Danny she knew, yet here he was treating her like an outcast—and because of Gerry Sovani too. It was Danny, not Susanna, who was behaving loosely. He was living openly with a woman. All Susanna had done was make one date with Gerry to try and forget her own loneliness. And that hadn't lasted long either, as soon as she had realised how incompatible they were. So Susanna sat at home and grieved in her heart, and wished she knew the secret of meditation.

Sunday evening dragged out, long and alone. She found herself dreading going back to the Pagoda now. She had looked forward to Danny's cheerfulness so much, his bantering remarks, his teasing. But he had changed since Caroline had come, that was clear. He was no longer the Danny they knew. She didn't want to go back and meet only the shell of the man she once so admired, the man who once had needed her so much . . .

She reached for the phone. 'Mrs Paw. Sorry to disturb you—'

'That okay, lah. Very grateful for all the good work you did in Brunei. My husband say to let you know you are getting a rise as from the end of this month.'

'That's nice, Mrs Paw.' But money didn't mean much

just now. 'Would it be too much trouble to take a week
of my holidays before I go back?'

Mrs Paw was in an expansive mood. 'Yes, sure you
can. Tilly can look after the place. She tell me she want
to make a few improvements while she is there.'

'Fine.' It might have annoyed her once, but now she
didn't mind if Tilly installed a hundred computers. All
she wanted was a few days so that she could pull herself
together, get into a firmer frame of mind, decide her
future. It was wrong to go back in her present state. She
knew she wouldn't be giving her work the concentration
it needed. Damn that man, for having such power over
her every move, her very existence. She had to get over
him fast—and the best way was to stay away from him
for a while.

She had an idea in her mind what to do today. She
dressed carefully in her white pleated skirt and dark blue
blouse. Work had been so much fun up to now. Now it
loomed over her like a monster, giving her no peace of
mind. She had longed for the Pagoda when she was out
in Brunei. Now she was nervous of setting foot there.

And so it was in the early afternoon that she walked
slowly and deliberately towards the great gold iron gates
of Lotus House—home of the legendary Mr Heng. She
knew she looked well. But she wanted to look more than
well. She had decided to come to the man whose life she
had saved, and ask him to give her a job—a job far from
Singapore, where she could devote herself to her career
without the presence of disturbing surgeons with green
eyes and curly hair . . . She took a deep breath. She must
look calm and mature, and give him a very good reason
for leaving such a good post in Singapore.

The waiting room was lavishly comfortable. As she
sat, a boy passed her three times with various newspapers and magazines. When he returned the third time
he was puffing, and he smiled at Susanna's expression of

sympathy. 'First time he want the Singapore papers. Then he wanted to know London and New York prices. This lot is from Tokyo and Sydney. And this is when he is under doctor's orders to take it easy.'

'I can see what it must be like when he's back to normal.'

The boy shrugged. 'Don't know how he keeps it up. My brother thinks he works by batteries.'

Susanna was still smiling after he had disappeared into a large room off to the left of them. She knew what made him tick—and she had been the one to get his heart going again. It was a good feeling. A manservant appeared silently before her. 'Follow me, Miss Valentine.' He led her to the double doors of white and gold where the boy had gone before. The handles shone, and she realised they must be real gold. The footman lowered his voice 'Madam—only ten minutes. Please remember he is not yet well.'

'I understand.'

The man opened both doors for her. 'Miss Valentine.'

Susanna entered the long sunny room. There was a polished wood floor, beautiful Chinese rugs and the walls were lined with books on two sides. Mr Heng sat in a white leather wheelchair, the newspapers the boy had brought piled on a table beside him. He looked up as she entered, and smiled into his chins like a jade Buddha.

'Come and sit here. What does a man say to the one who saved his life?'

Susanna went forward and shook his hand, then sat down on a chair with a satin embroidered seat and back, the ends of the arms carved in gold. She felt awed by the very size and beauty of the room, the items in it crying out their cost almost beyond belief. She tried to answer his question. 'I suppose it was just lucky I was there at the time.'

He nodded. 'More than lucky. A miracle I can never forget.'

'Anyone with my training could have done the same.'

The great man smiled again. 'Miss Valentine, I have already thanked Dr Sovani in my own way. Please accept a similar gift—in return for the gift of my life.' He picked up a long envelope that was lying beside the papers. 'There is a cheque inside.'

She gasped. 'Oh but—I didn't come for—it's good of you, but that isn't why I came.'

He wasn't angry. 'You refuse money? That is curious. It makes you a rather special young woman, you know.' His voice was deep and fatherly. She couldn't imagine him at that moment as a businessman. He was a cross between Santa Claus and Buddha.

Encouraged by his manner, she said, 'No, sir, I'm very ordinary. But I didn't come here for a reward. I helped you because you were ill, not because you were rich.'

'But why refuse when I can thank you with money?'

'I'd rather have a job.' She blurted out the words. Of course, she would have liked the money as well, but in her present state of mind, she knew that getting away from Danny was all she wanted. Mr Heng was in a position to help her do that. He had a large enough empire to find her a job similar to the one she had.

'That wouldn't be difficult. But Ellen Paw is a good friend of mine, and I know she treasures you highly. I would feel it was wrong to poach you away from her. There would have to be a very good reason.' There. That was the question she was dreading. How could she expect him to understand? How could she be honest, and still retain his respect? He leaned forward, and went on, 'I'm not making difficulties, you understand. But if this is just an emotional problem, Miss Valentine, how will I know that you will stick at any other job if you have another problem of the heart?'

Susanna paused. She must choose her words very carefully. He was right, and her explanation had to be credible. 'I am sure that this is an exceptional position I'm in. I don't lack loyalty to Mrs Paw, truly. But this—er—attachment—is one that won't crop up again, I'm sure of that.' Had that worked? Attachment was a mild word for the tempest inside her, but she had to sound sensible, to show that she knew what she wanted.

He looked at her with his narrow, kindly eyes. 'Ah so.'

In the ensuing silence there was a heart-rendingly beautiful outburst of birdsong. A servant had opened a slatted door and walked out into the lush garden with a pail of water and a basket of birdseed. The birds of all colours fluttered and hopped, a brilliant kaleidoscope in the sun, whirling against the dark green backcloth of the trees and shrubs. Susanna sighed. The world of nature here seemed so simple and untroubled by tensions. Even the squabbling of the birds appeared playful.

She turned back to Mr Heng. 'I'm taking your time, sir. You must be tired.'

'One moment more. You must not go empty-handed.'

'I'm not. I'm taking away the peace and gentleness of your lovely garden. I sat next to a man on a plane who told me that he was successful because he was tranquil.'

'Really? I am opposite. I am tranquil because I was successful enough to buy this house.' His smile was definitely inscrutable. Susanna looked at him, puzzled, and he said quickly, 'Miss Valentine, perhaps I can help you—even give you what you most desire. Do you think I can?'

'The job, you mean?'

'Peace of mind. Philosophy.'

She gave a smile, half-understanding. 'If I stay at the Pagoda?'

'Give it a try.'

'But how can you do that?'

'Not I. These.' And he indicated with a wide sweep of his hand in its loose oriental sleeve, the two walls of books. 'Take what you like. Spend time here—as much as you wish. My books and my garden are at your disposal.'

Susanna wasn't sure why, but she felt greatly honoured. 'Am I bright enough to learn from them, sir?'

'Oh yes. You have heard of the Chinese belief in yin/yang? The total equality of opposites?'

'There is no equality between sense and nonsense, is there?'

At this, the comfortable figure before her burst into genuine laughter. 'Oh, my dear Miss Valentine, you will learn very quickly. Go now, and find out.' He tinkled a silver bell at his elbow, almost hidden by the pile of newspapers.

And in the next few hours, Susanna did find out quite a lot. The librarian was a tall woman with straight iron-grey hair. Her name was Miss Koh. In the short afternoon she communicated to her guest all the huge enthusiasm for the books in her care. They talked non-stop, pausing only for jasmine tea, served in a silver pot, in a small summerhouse covered all over with creeper and honeysuckle.

'Confucius isn't all that difficult.'

Miss Koh poured more tea into the tiny bowls, and agreed quietly with a nod and a smile. 'To me he is a real friend.' They walked for a while in the garden before Susanna felt that she ought to leave. Miss Koh made it clear that she looked forward to seeing her again.

Susanna walked home not seeing the Singapore streets, but a blaze of beauty and contentment. Mr Heng had indeed given her much more than money. Her sadness was now less acute. She accepted now what Danny had once said to her and Mei Li—'Don't be afraid of living.' In a way, she now knew that he was right. She found that now she didn't resent what had happened between them. When they had made love it was because, at that moment, they did indeed mean so much to each other. She couldn't doubt Danny's sincerity any more. She couldn't regret that it was he who had turned her into a woman. There was still the ache in her heart, knowing that he did not belong to her. But it would fade, that ache, in the course of kindly time . . .

She presented herself at Lotus House next morning early but Miss Koh was waiting and glad of her company. They spent almost all day together, though after lunch, served in the summerhouse, Susanna was left for a while to wander as she wished. She felt the serenity seeping into her soul. Time didn't seem to matter in this particular Eden. The smells, sights and sounds filled her with calm and quiet joy.

As she said good night, the darkness was almost falling, the sun low behind the travellers' palms outlined on the horizon. 'I think I'm looking forward to the Pagoda now,' she confided to Miss Koh. 'Mr Heng was very clever to see that I didn't really want to leave. I saved his life—but he's given me back my pleasure in life.' She didn't spell it out to the kindly woman, but what she meant was that she knew she could face Danny now—wanted to face him, and to carry on living even though Life hadn't given her all she asked for.

But that evening tested her new-found peace far harder than she was willing to be tested. There was a ring at the doorbell. She was relaxing over a cup of coffee in the kitchen, dressed in a cotton housecoat, her hair dishevelled round her face. Her oriental serenity flew out of the window, as she looked up into the green eyes. 'Oh—Danny—hello—'

'Hello.' His voice told her nothing. His eyes were

searching her outline, and she pulled the sash of her robe tighter. Suddenly she was reminded of that flaxen-haired girl Danny held in his memory—and knew that at the moment she came close to his image. His voice was a shade deeper when he added, 'I'm sorry for coming unannounced. But it was important.'

'Would you like to come in?'

'Please.'

She stood aside. He walked into the flat, bringing with him his distinctive presence, odour, reassurance—and the memories that she knew of that night he had stayed —the night she would never forget.

'Look, I know you are on holiday. Tell me now if you want me to go. I already feel like a heel.'

She said quickly, 'Oh no. I'm glad to see you.' It was difficult to be welcoming without sounding besotted. She thought 'Glad' was the right word. She followed him into the lounge. 'Would you like some coffee?' The memory of his furious expression that night at Dr Roy's house lingered in the background. There was no sign of that now.

He turned to face her. Suddenly her heart was fluttering like one of Mr Heng's caged canaries. Lotus House had indeed helped her to think straight, but it had no effect at all on the chemical reaction that flooded her with a glow of physical response to her nearness. 'Susanna—I came to ask you a favour.'

'About Bas?' She had a feeling that he might force her to intervene. And she knew her loyalty to the boy would stop her. For all her overwhelming affection, she couldn't let Bas down.

'No. Not Bas. A patient. You don't know him.'

'But . . .'

Danny took her hands in his. 'Please? It's a serious case. Mr Lin—an art teacher—a calligrapher—famous all round Singapore. His sight is going—a tumour. I think it's benign—but what good is that if you can't earn your living after the operation? I'm operating tomorrow morning.'

'Why do you want me? Sister Silvano is good. Very good. She's had years of experience.'

'Older doesn't mean wiser, Valentine. It's you I need.' He increased the pressure of his hands. 'And so does he, believe me.'

'Put like that . . .'

'Bless you, Valentine.'

She looked into his eyes. It was a luxury, but she couldn't help it. 'It used to infuriate me when you called me that. But I'm glad now. It's—sort of friendly.'

'Right. It matters to you?'

She couldn't lie to him. 'Yes.'

There was a slight pause. He let her hands go. 'Do you mind if I sit down?'

'Of course not.'

He sat for a moment, looking down. Susanna sat opposite, waiting. He faced her when he started to speak. 'Tilly tells me you're leaving us. I know it's no business of mine—but don't be reckless about your life. The Pagoda really needs you, you know. It wouldn't be the same without you.'

'They'll manage.'

'Gerry will miss you.'

Susanna frowned slightly. 'I'll miss him. I'll miss everyone.'

'Specially Gerry?'

'For heaven's sake, Danny—you don't have a right to grill me . . .'

'Sorry.' His eyes were suddenly alarmed, as though he regretted losing her goodwill. 'He's not a bad chap. Talented, good-looking, good at his job. Suits you really.'

Susanna looked stern. 'Danny Redfearn, it is nothing

at all to do with you, but have you ever heard of just good friends?'

He turned away. After a moment he said, 'I've no right at all to go on at you like that. I'm sorry again.' She couldn't retain her anger. She looked down at him with a mixture of concern and longing. He said without looking up, 'Was Caroline at the nightclub you went to with Gerry?'

Susanna hated telling tales. But she also couldn't lie. 'She might have been. Why do you ask?'

'She said she wasn't. But other people have told me. I believe she was rather drunk.'

Susanna was hesitant. 'A bit. But she must have been missing you.'

Danny stood up. His actions were abrupt, but it was impossible to read his face. She watched him, her own forehead wrinkled with concern. 'Are you sure you wouldn't like some coffee?'

'Coffee, Valentine, is what I don't need right now.' He turned to face her. He looked down until she faced him, eye to eye. 'Shall I tell you what I do need?'

He was very close. She felt the force of his personality, that felt as though it belonged to her. Almost all of herself wanted to give in, to take him into her arms, as she knew he wanted too. The night was sultry, tense with unspoken yearnings . . . She spoke rapidly, almost warding him away—'You need a theatre sister for tomorrow morning. I'll be there.'

For the first time there was a trace of a smile on his face. She loved him even more when his eyes crinkled up like that. 'Who but my Valentine would be so very definite?'

My Valentine . . . The words fell on her ears like honey. But the idea of Caroline was too close. She answered briskly, 'I am the Administrator. It's my job.'

'How could I forget it?' He took a step away, but

paused. Then he used her name, and it turned her knees
to water. 'Susanna—' his voice deepened, 'You have
a very lovely tender heart under your dragonly exterior.
I'm proud—very proud—of being able to call you my
friend. You realise that?'

She swallowed. This was a burst of honesty that left
her reeling. 'No.' More words wouldn't come. She could
tell that at a sign from her, he would stay. The words
were unspoken, but clear. There was respect there, for
her and for her protection of Bas. He couldn't say it
more clearly. His admiration was not conditional on
helping him to find Bas. He cared for her—period.
Tears oozed into her eyes as she realised the extent of his
regard. 'Oh Danny . . .'

He held her then very tightly. It was brief and very
close. It helped them both. She was glad she had the
strength to let him go. That relieved them both of any
extra entanglement that could do no more good . . . As
he let her free, he whispered, 'Thanks for saying you'll
come.'

After he had gone, she cried a little. It wasn't going to
be easy, but she would be working with him again. She
knew she must. Better to be at the Pagoda, with all its
heartache, than to be exiled to Brunei. She had Mr Heng
to thank for that.

Mei Li wasn't even there in the morning when
Susanna arrived. No matter. She walked out at the back.
She would get changed in good time. The Japanese
garden was pretty, still spangled with a few drops of dew.
If she hadn't been here, she would have been going to
the fabulous gardens of Lotus House. She looked down
at the tiny stream. It was insignificant beside the tranquil
beauty of the lake at Mr Heng's with its painted ducks
and geese, parading like an ancient landscape in one of
his priceless books.

'Good morning. Thank you for coming.' She heard

the lapping of the tiny stream as she looked up to see
Danny, tall, erect, confident. But his greeting was less
than chirpy. 'I appreciate it, you know.'

She saw the tension of the coming operation in his
face. 'I'm glad to help.'

'It's a bad one. Can I show you the angiogram? It's his
sight. He teaches calligraphy—brilliant at it, famous all
over the country—I told you last night. If his sight goes,
he's finished. Even if I remove the tumour, he has no life
without his eyes.'

'Both eyes equally?'

'Yes. The tumour is central. A meningioma.'

'After operation, you still won't be sure, then?'

'No . . . There's always the threat of haemorrhage. Or
fits. The first few hours are crucial.'

'You do have faith in your nurses?'

'Yes, thank God. And I've got you. That's another
plus.'

Susanna was silent. Even his conventional remarks
made her want him. She must stop this. He belonged,
clearly, to Caroline Moore. Susanna took a deep breath.
Nothing mattered this morning but that one patient, and
the ordeal through which he and Danny would travel
together. She said, 'Shall we go? The angiogram you
were going to show me?'

He didn't move. 'Yes. He's a sweet old man.' There
was about a foot between them. She could feel the heat
from his body. 'I've talked to him. He has a lot of faith in
me.' He brushed his fingers through his hair, nervously
—and reminded Susanna very much of Bas.

In a gentle voice she said, 'We all have.'

Diffident, he said, 'Susanna—I wish you knew—
there's so much we have to talk about . . . I think I said
the wrong thing last night . . . No, not wrong—maybe
too much . . .'

Now was not the time for personalities, sweet though

they might be. Susanna said in a business-like voice, 'You came last night to ask me to come in for this one operation. I agreed. Here I am. Shall we go?'

He nodded, but didn't move. 'Just one thing—I actually came last night to apologise for being so rude at Roy's party. I don't know why I did it, and I felt you would wonder what had come over me.'

She said quietly, 'Thinking back, I think I was probably more rude than you.'

'With every justification.'

The birds sang around them. They stood talking together in the miniature garden. Anyone watching them would have seen none of the tension and uncertainty—only two figures who seemed to fit together so well, work together so well . . . .

'Danny—' and she heard him draw in his breath when she said his name. He faced her. She knew now why he was apologising. He wanted the atmosphere in theatre to be friendly and co-operative. She knew as well as he that it wasn't in the patient's interest for there to be any tension between colleagues. This operation was far too important for him to take any chances. And Susanna was a good enough nurse to know that Danny was right. She smiled as naturally as possible. 'Okay, so we've both apologised and both apologies accepted, right?'

'I do hope so.' He stood to one side then, and she walked past him towards the door to the hospital. 'Thanks, Valentine.' At the door he said, 'Come through. I'll show you those tests before we change. Then you'll know just what we're taking on this morning.'

Yet in spite of the gravity of the situation, she was glad to hear that his voice was almost back to its confident, jaunty self. It was almost as though he had grown taller as they walked. Just because she had been sensible and helped him to make the atmosphere calm.

Susanna smiled to herself. After the operation she could be as cutting as she wanted. She could send him back to his dear Caroline with a flea in his ear. Coming smarming over her just for the sake of one operation indeed! Charm was Danny's middle name, and she ought to have known that by now.

Yet somehow the sight of those angiograms, and the CT scan, wiped the smile off her face. Danny Redfearn had a job and a half in front of him. The tumour was so large that it was a miracle poor Mr Lin was still alive, and had in fact been teaching up to the previous week, when his sight let him down at an important occasion.

'Okay, Valentine?'

'Yes. I'll go and scrub.'

'Think we can do it?'

She smiled, forcing the words. 'You are Danny Redfearn, aren't you? Of course we can do it.'

CHAPTER TWELVE

GOWNED and masked, Susanna entered the Theatre.
The instruments were there sterile and shining. She
collected those that would be required and placed them
as neatly as possible in the order they would be needed.
Of course Danny would operate the electric saw himself,
but she made sure the power was on, and that the switch
under his foot was in instant working order. Swabs,
dressings, sutures—everything was rechecked with
Nurse Fallon. She had done her part. Jo-Jo was with the
patient now outside the Theatre, discussing his job, to
keep him relaxed until Danny was ready. Dr Nye was
with them too, reading once more through the notes,
checking the CT scan and the angiogram that Danny had
been over with them already. The atmosphere was
hushed and grave—but not upsetting. They were all
well-trained. They were doing the job to the best of their
ability. No false note of undue emotion or stress would
intrude while the operation was going on. Quiet confidence that all would be well—that was all they must
feel now.

Danny arrived, and shook the patient's hand. 'Right,
Mr Lin. You are all Dr Chou's now.' Jo-Jo took the left
hand, and injected the pentothal.

Mr Lin smiled as the needle went in. *'Terimakasih.'*
And then his eyelids drooped, his consciousness slipped
quietly away. They all knew that when those eyes
opened again they might not see. But there was nothing
but calm confidence in Danny Redfearn's voice as he
preceded the trolley into Theatre. 'Okay for the
halothane, Jo-Jo.'

172

'Ready, Danny. He's all yours.'

Danny turned his head towards Susanna. The green gaze met the blue one. 'Ready, Sister?' She handed him the battery shaver without being asked. Danny removed what was left of the old man's greying fuzz of hair. 'Iodine. Scalpel.' He made a clean confident cut just above the forehead. Then, with the CT scan clearly fixed where he could see it without craning his neck, he took the cutter from Susanna. The high-pitched burr of bone being cut filled the little Theatre.

It took almost five hours. There was little talk while the operation was going on. Concentration had to be keen, and everyone followed the surgeon's every move. It was almost two-fifteen. The team had stood around the recumbent man, moving their feet in the white boots only when they felt stiff in the same position. Hands and arms, and the gleam of stainless steel, were the only moving parts in this dramatic tableau.

There was a small bustle as the bleeding threatened to swamp the field. Susanna was ready, at a fractional nod from Danny, to swab as soon as Dr Nye had moved the suction tube. Neatly, unobtrusively as she could. Danny asked, 'How many pints did we get out of the fridge?'

'You asked for six.'

'Get another couple, please.'

Nurse Fallon went at a sign from Susanna. He might have been asking for half-a-dozen eggs at the grocers. The calm was not disturbed, and the bleeding gradually got under control.

'That is pretty good.' Danny was congratulating himself as all the dangerous tissue was removed. 'They know I want the histology results as fast as they can.' He bent to look carefully into the cavity. Susanna reached out with a pad, and caught the beads of sweat that were threatening to run into his eyes. 'Thank you, Valentine.' He looked up. There was almost a twinkle in his eye.

That—and the use of her name instead of 'Sister' meant that his tension was lessening now. The worst was over.

Nye ventured a comment. 'There doesn't seem to be any damage.'

'I don't think there is. Almost like shelling peas, isn't it, Dr Nye?'

'Possibly, Dr Redfearn. Sooner you than me.'

'Sometimes the larger ones are easier at the time. Depends how much surrounding tissue is involved.' He took a small step back from the table, and stretched his back, and shoulders. Susanna meanwhile mopped gently at the cavity left by the mass he had removed. 'Thanks, Valentine.' He came back to the patient. 'Now this is the time when you might get complacent, but don't ever do that, Nye. He can be back in the ward, and we can all be congratulating ourselves when, whoosh! One single convulsion, one tiny haemorrhage—and it's all ruined. So say your prayers for him now. It would be a great pity if all our work was for nothing.'

He started to close the wound. 'Over to you, God.' He sounded flippant, but Susanna knew he meant it—they all did. As the final stitches were knotted, she suddenly felt the tiredness that had not affected any of them during the operation. Muscles felt sore, eyes gritty. One by one they stood back as Jo-Jo removed the tube, and Dr Nye completed the bandaging with a drainage tube. Blood was set up and a glucose saline drip. Finally Jo-Jo gave the signal to return him gently to Intensive Care, where the oxygen was to be connected.

Susanna stood for a while in the empty theatre after she had checked that all the instruments and swabs were present. It was so quiet now. The clock said almost three o'clock—she had missed seeing Mr Heng's lake at its best in the mid-afternoon sun. But it didn't bother her. She was glad she had been here, glad that she had been able to use her skills to the full in yet another human

drama. She would go to the ward to see him wake. The
routine miracle. But she felt a sort of lift every time a
patient came round having been made well. Pulling off
her mask, she followed the trolley without changing her
Theatre clothes.

The oxygen mask was over most of Mr Lin's face.
His eyes were open, and there was tension round the
bed as he turned slightly, recognising Danny. 'Oh, Dr
Redfearn. I've been to the moon.'

There was a broad smile on Danny's face as he
replied, 'And come back safely, Mr Lin. To the moon
and back. Not bad in one morning.' He turned to Dr
Nye. 'Thank you, young man.' He looked for Susanna.
'Thank you, Sister Valentine.' Then he beckoned the
Recovery nurse to commence monitoring. As he passed
Susanna he said, 'I'd be awfully grateful if you could stay
for just a short time. I know I can rely on you to say the
right thing.'

'All right.' She didn't mind. She could go to Lotus
House later. And she did want to watch over him for a
while. At this stage every patient is unique, and Susanna
had been through it so recently with Lucy Ming. She sat
at the desk, while the nurse checked blood pressure and
pupil reaction. Danny left the ward. For a few minutes
there was only Susanna and the nurse. Then a voice
came from the bed, muffled by the oxygen mask, 'If you
weren't in that ugly old gown I'd think you were an
angel. Your hair is such a beautiful colour.'

Susanna went over to Mr Lin's bed. She smiled down
at him. 'With tubes at every orifice and a few extra, you
can lie there and pay compliments, Mr Lin.'

'You can't know what it's like. My sight was failing.
Now it is so clear, Sister. The sunlight is like heavenly
glory. And your hair is the most beautiful gold. I feel
almost euphoric. I want to get up and sing and dance
with the happiness.'

'I hope you can postpone the dancing for a day or two. But believe me, we'd all like to join in.'

The little nurse came back. 'Excuse me, Sister. Can I do his blood pressure again.'

Susanna stood back. But as the thin brown arm was bared for its routine examination, he reached out and took her hand. 'Thank you, Sister.' She smiled at him. As soon as the tests were done, he closed his eyes and slept. Her job was done. The afternoon sun was strong, and she closed the blind a little more before she left. She heard the nurse wake him long enough to do the final check.

'And where are you, Mr Lin?'

His voice was drowsy but firm. 'The Pagoda Hospital on the twenty-eighth of August. And it feels like Paradise because I'm surrounded by angels.'

The little nurse dimpled as she filled in the chart. She saw Susanna still at the door. 'There are times when I quite like this job.'

She was glad that she did not see Danny Redfearn again as she made her way out. She used the Hospital exit, rather than cross the Japanese garden. It meant a longer walk home, but she didn't want to risk meeting him again. Having done a most satisfying day's work, all Susanna wanted was to get back to her holiday, which so far had been such fun and such a help.

Apart from paying a happy visit to Lucy Ming, she spent the rest of her days—Wednesday, Thursday and Friday—at Lotus House, absorbing not only philosophy, but quiet peace and beauty. She did not see Mr Heng again, but Miss Koh said that he would see her at once if she wished it. She knew that he wanted her to stay in Mrs Paw's employment. Indeed, it was a great compliment for Mrs Paw to want her so much. Perhaps Tilly had made it clear that she had become bored with the Pagoda as a toy.

'I'll be back at the Pagoda on Monday.'

Miss Koh poured the tea. Such a polite, civilised fragrance. Susanna lifted her small handleless cup with two hands. 'But you will visit me again?'

'I do hope so.' Susanna set her cup down before gesturing around the lovely garden. 'I never knew such a place was hiding in the heart of the city.'

'I will be happy to make you welcome. In your lunch hour perhaps?'

'That would be lovely.' Susanna thought to herself that after a harrowing morning she would be delighted to have permission to come to such a place.

'From what you told me of Mr Lin, the Pagoda has a need of you.'

'I need it too. I've done so much to build it up.'

'Then call when you can. Even if I am busy Mr Heng has made it clear that you have access to his house at all times.'

'He is sweet.'

Miss Koh looked at her through her spectacles, raising her eyebrows. 'He is clever. He is just. He is—on occasions—kind.'

'And sweet,' insisted Susanna.

Miss Koh smiled. She lifted her tiny cup in salute. 'To a happy return to the Pagoda, Susanna.'

On Monday she was at her desk early. She lifted the appointment book, and opened its broad pages. She knew she was glad to be back. The very fountain seemed to spurt out a welcome, the tiny drops falling with a happy, optimistic sound. Susanna swung her head, enjoying the feel of her new loose hairstyle under the lace cap. Danny Redfearn had done her no favours, but he had planted the seed of the idea. The girl with the flaxen hair. She felt free and natural, having no pins to bother about. She bent to the page with a smile. All these entries in untidy handwriting! It would soon be obvious that the Administrator-in-chief was back.

'Oh thank goodness. What a wonderful sight.' Mei Li wasn't exactly late, but she ran in with a smile on her face. 'I hated being in charge. Not for all six of them. It was too much.'

'But they were nice to you. My doctors are always nice.'

'Of course. But they do have high standards. That's all your doing.' She flung her handbag down. 'Shall I make you a cup of tea?'

'Please. I'd love jasmine.'

'Jasmine? That's new. Since your holiday?'

'I'll tell you all about it at lunch.'

Mei Li put the kettle on. 'I'll tell you, Susanna, I was so scared when Tilly told us you might go and work for the Bandar Seri Begawan Clinic. My heart sank to my feet.'

'That was one of Tilly's ideas. She didn't tell me.'

'Now I know it. But then I was really miserable.'

'Tilly didn't exactly cheer anyone up.'

'She may not come in this week, now that we're back to normal.'

Normal. That was a good word. One that made Susanna smile, now that she had talked over such things with Miss Koh. She sipped at the scented tea. 'Now —why is there a crooked line across Dr Redfearn's morning?'

'Oh—he won't be in. And it's meant to be a straight line.'

'I see.' Susanna pretended to be strict. 'Well, Mother's back now!'

'Oh gosh.' Mei Li gave her a cheerful wave as she pulled the cover from her machine.

Gerry's first patient came in. 'I'm afraid you are here before Dr Sovani.'

'It doesn't matter. I don't mind waiting.'

Susanna directed her to the dental section. Then she gave Gerry a welcoming grin as he came trotting up the steps. 'This one was in a hurry.'

He stopped and smiled at her. 'How good you look. Now I know everything will go smoothly today.'

'Don't count on it.' But it was a joke. Everyone was glad she was back at the helm. After Gerry had gone she said to Mei Li, 'Why isn't Danny in today?'

'Busy at home. He's coming later. About two, he said.'

'Oh.'

'You don't still love that man?'

'Not a lot.' She turned the conversation swiftly. 'What do you know of yin/yang, Mei Li?'

'Opposites. Male and female.'

'Is that all?'

'Of course not.' She went back to her typewriter. 'Do you really still love him?'

'I guess so. But it will wear off. Don't worry, I'll survive.' She told Mei Li something of Lotus House during lunch hour. Her enthusiasm was such that her friend was begging to be taken along too. Susanna had to agree to mention it.

She missed seeing Danny that afternoon. He couldn't have planned it, so it was just luck that she was not at her desk when he arrived. And when he left, it was just at the moment when Susanna decided to ask Mei Li why Tilly Paw was not in.

'She's preparing for the next stage in her education. She's going to manage a fashion house in Hong Kong.'

'That sounds more Tilly than being nursemaid to six doctors.'

'She said it had been quite an experience.'

Susanna smiled. 'I expect the yin/yang wasn't in its proper proportions for her.'

'You had better be careful about all this science. A little learning is a dangerous thing, Susanna.'

Susanna was looking for something to throw that wouldn't leave a bruise on her young friend's delicate skin, when the telephone purred. 'At this hour?' But she dutifully picked it up. 'Hello?'

'Susanna. Tilly Paw.'

'Hello, Tilly. Lucky you. I've just been told about your great future in Fashion.'

'Oh that.'

'You aren't sure?'

'I don't know. But I'd like to see you. Can you meet me at the Raffles Bar? Ahmad will bring you.'

Susanna didn't have any arrangements. 'All right. I'll come along.' But it was strange. Tilly had spent her time trying to get the better of Susanna. Why did she want a friendly drink together?

Before she left, she went to the Hospital to see Mr Lin. He was still euphoric, cute in his delight at everything about him. 'Sometimes I wonder if perhaps everyone ought to go through this kind of ordeal. Nothing makes a person so gloriously happy to be on this planet with all senses in working order.'

'Don't say that, Mr Lin. There aren't enough Danny Redfearns to go around.'

'That's very true. What a man. What a profession.'

Susanna smiled as she left him. 'It's wonderful to know you will be going back to your profession.'

'I will, I will. And every minute in it will be deeply felt.' Susanna went away feeling humble, that one human being could make such a difference to another. Danny had many grateful patients. Yet—ruefully she had to admit—she must be the one human being he did not want to help. Yet he was the only medical man who could do anything about her heart problem . . . Life could be so ironic.

Ahmad was waiting in the foyer, chatting to Rahman, the doorkeeper. Susanna walked down the steps into the twilight. 'To the Raffles, please.' And as she stepped into the cool air-conditioned limousine, she wondered how many times he had taken Danny and Tilly there. But Tilly was bowing out now. Susanna always knew she would. A surgeon was too dedicated to his work. Tilly wasn't the kind of woman who liked being ignored —even for a good cause. And as the Mercedes purred towards Raffles City, Susanna found herself wondering if Bridget Redfearn had been a bit like Tilly? She might have expected more from her husband than a doctor can give. His time is spent with his patients. And when he gets home he needs sympathy and understanding, not complaints about the washing machine, or the boredom of staying in the house all day. She had seen it before. Danny's story sounded much the same. But it was no concern of hers.

The Raffles was its usual fresh white self—known the world over in history books and tales of the Second World War. Now it basked in the evening moon, refined and dignified like some elderly but beautiful duchess. The tall palms at the door soared into the dark blue sky on slim stems. The travellers palms were floodlit, their elegant fan shapes making semicircular shadows on the white exterior of the hotel. Behind it the modern blocks of flats and offices were lit high into the stars. But here in this three-storey colonial style history lesson Tilly Paw was sitting at the Long Bar. She was chatting to one of the barmen. Susanna smiled to herself. Tilly was a hard-headed businesswoman, but she could never resist a compliment.

Tilly saw her approaching. 'Susanna. You look so very smart.'

'Thank you.' She had worn her favourite linen shift in dusty pink. It showed off her slim tanned arms, and she had some matching shoes and a shoulder bag. Her hair swung, light and shining, and she knew she looked well. A woman can tell when glances are flattering, even though she pretends she cannot notice the admiring faces. She went to the bar and took the next stool to Tilly. Two pink gin slings were already poured out, the ice cubes melting but not yet invisible. 'Cheers.'

'I wanted to say goodbye. I'm off to Hong Kong next weekend.'

'Lots of luck. Mei Li told me it was fashion. You'll be a natural.'

'I don't know how you can be so nice to me.'

Susanna put her glass down. 'What on earth do you mean?'

'Well—I asked you here so that I can apologise.'

'I don't recall any reason.'

'You must have wondered why you went to Brunei on your own?'

Susanna smiled, setting the other girl at ease. 'No. You wanted to get Danny on his own. I didn't wonder, I knew.'

Tilly looked very relieved. 'You don't mind then?' Susanna didn't reply. 'It served me right. He hardly spoke to me the whole week.'

'Well he wouldn't, would he? He must have been missing Caroline.'

'Caroline?' Tilly looked surprised. 'Caroline is the last person he'd miss. You mean to say you don't know?'

'All I know about Caroline is that she wears blue a lot, she drinks too much, and she lives with Danny.'

'No no. You've got it wrong. At least—partly wrong. He took her to the airport on Monday. Didn't you notice he took the morning off? She followed him here when she got back on drugs. She was a cousin of his wife. He'd paid for a detoxification clinic in London a few years ago. When she got back on cocaine—not difficult if you want to—she flew out here and asked him to help her again.'

'Did he tell you all this himself?'

'Yes. Well he had to. She turned up out of the blue, clinging on to him and telling him he was the only person who could help her. He gave her three weeks to pull herself together. She didn't.'

'I noticed,' Susanna said drily.

'Right. So he paid for her flight back—and arranged for the Clinic in London to pick her up and take her back for intensive residential treatment.'

Susanna sipped the last of her drink. Tilly's revelations had been worth coming for. 'Poor chap.'

'He hasn't had it easy.'

Susanna felt suddenly weepy. 'He doesn't complain.'

'Right.'

'So why did you think I ought to know all this?'

Tilly beckoned the barman, who brought two replacements. 'Partly because of my own conscience. When I came to the Pagoda—I was prepared to despise you. I thought I was so well-educated that I had to be your superior.' She said quietly, 'I'm not, Susanna. Thanks for teaching me.'

'I didn't do anything.'

Tilly smiled. 'I know. But somehow you made me feel a hell of a heel. We should have gone to Brunei together. We'd have straightened the place up—and had a good time. As it was—Danny said nothing, and it rained!'

'I can see that wasn't a load of laughs.'

'Ah well—Hong Kong here I come. What about you Susanna?'

'I'm back in harness. It's good.'

'And—?'

'Well, my head is still spinning about Caroline Moore.'

'What do you think Danny will do now?'

Susanna thought, looking deep into the depths of her glass. 'He once told me he had no home. I wouldn't be surprised if he moved on. He mentioned Australia once.'

'That would be a terrible waste. The Pagoda needs him, Susanna.'

Susanna smiled. 'That wouldn't bother him. He's his own man. No one can change his mind.' She faced her attractive companion. 'We'll miss him.'

'That is the understatement of the century. Why don't you go to him—now that you know Caroline meant nothing? Persuade him that Singapore is the place to be.'

Susanna said again, 'He's his own man. Only he can decide.'

'You could help.'

She shook her head. 'I doubt it. If his own heart doesn't tell him to stay—then I'm not going to bully him.'

'For goodness sake—and I thought you were—oh well, never mind.' She held out her hand. 'Cheerio, Susanna. I'll come and see you when I come home, shall I?'

Susanna smiled. 'Please do. I won't be moving.' They shook hands.

Ahmad was waiting to take Susanna home. 'Thank you for waiting. You must want to get back home.'

'No. I like my work. Home is small—boring. This way I get to see all the real plushy places. I used to stay for Miss Tilly somtimes till ten, eleven. I don't mind.' He said in a confiding tone, 'She never did get that Dr Redfearn to do what she want!'

Susanna didn't answer. It was almost nine when she got back to her flat. She pushed open the door and kicked off her shoes. She was hungry, but lazy to cook. The Silver Swan was the ready answer. After a shower and a change of clothes, she'd go there. But there was a scent in the air—newly boiled rice, frying onions . . .

'Hi Susanna. It's only me.'

'Sebastian Redfearn!'

She expected him to deny the name. But he didn't. 'You don't mind me coming back?'

'My dear, of course not. Lucy said she hadn't seen you for a while. They were worried.'

'Were you?'

'No. I missed you. But I knew you could take care of yourself.'

'You like some prawn chow mein?'

'There's nothing in the world I'd like better. Have I time to shower?'

'Oh yes. I haven't sliced up my secret ingredient yet.' He put his hand in his jeans pocket. 'Sue, have a look at this. Lucy gave it me.' It was a photograph. It showed a good-looking couple holding a small tousle-headed toddler. 'That's me. Look on the back.' There was written 'Sebastian Redfearn—and doting parents' in Danny's hand.

'What does this prove? I told you he loved you.'

'I think this is the reason Lucy chose Dad when her doctor gave her several names of neurologists to choose from. This photo was in her album. When she pasted it in, she must have read the name on the back. All those years ago, and the name came back to her.'

Susanna smiled her assent. 'And you don't seem quite so anti-Redfearn as you used to be.'

'Don't get me wrong, Sue. I still don't need him, but I don't hate him. Is that a fair compromise?'

'Only if you'll consent to meet him.'

'No. Definitely no. No point.'

Susanna gave up. 'I'll go and shower.'

It was half an hour later when she returned to the lounge, dressed in a respectable but cool cotton housecoat. Delicious smells were emanating from the kitchen. Susanna opened the fridge, looking for something cold to drink. 'Sebastian, we've no lemonade left.'

'I'm sorry. I had the last. Hang on. I'll put this on a low heat and run out to the Plaza to get you some.'

'Thanks. It must be those gin slings. I feel terribly thirsty.'

'Only be five minutes.'

She leaned back on the sofa and put her feet up. And at that moment the doorbell rang. It was too soon for Bas. Susanna opened the door.

Danny stood there. 'Is it all right to speak to you?' His voice was cool, controlled.

'Yes, Danny. Come in.'

'I'm not in the way, am I? You have no other gentlemen callers?'

'Now what is that supposed to mean.' She stopped, suddenly hurt at the tone of his insinuations.

'Only that I was told you had a man here. And I wouldn't want to spoil your fun.'

Her heart had been calm up to then. But when she realised that he must have seen the figure of Bas leaving the flat, she felt suddenly very happy. They would meet. They had to now. She turned towards him and her smile was warm and genuine. 'Oh Danny, come and sit down. It's only chow mein, but you're welcome to share it. There's plenty.'

He came in, but he didn't sit down. And she saw that he was trying to find words to say. She wanted to take him in her arms. But it would not be proper. He said slowly, 'You know I came to Singapore to find my family.'

'Yes I know.'

'Do you remember me saying I had no home?'

'I'll always remember that.'

Something in her soft tone reached him. He went to

her, held her in his arms while he said the rest of his speech—haltingly now, and without any pretensions. 'Susanna—I never wanted to involve anyone else in my miserable pilgrimage. But I met you—and if I told you that where you are is home to me, would you understand what I was trying to say?'

She only had to whisper, because his head was so very close to hers. 'I would know. I do know. And if you'll let me, I'd like to prove it true.'

He kissed her, gently and lingeringly. He smoothed his hand over her hair, and let his fingers play with the silver-gold strands. 'I just want to be with you. Do you honestly not mind?'

She pushed him gently to sit down. As he sat in the corner of the sofa looking up at her she said, 'I'll work on it, Danny. I think maybe in a week or two I might be able to stand the sight of you.'

He had slipped easily into her bantering tone now, and she saw the beloved eyes begin to shine in the way she had always loved. Those eyes deep as the ocean . . .

'Darling girl. Come to me, Susanna. Come to me, love.'

She went to him because she had no will left to tease him with. She held him with a grip so tight that he could hardly breathe. 'Danny. Danny, I love you so much.'

He murmured, 'So my wanderings are over. I still can't believe it, love, but here is home—and it's so sweet and lovely. I can't leave you tonight, Susanna. I can't leave you ever. You won't turn me out of my only home, will you, love?'

'Never.' And she held him, understanding.

Suddenly his body tensed, his arms stiffened. 'What the hell is that?'

'What's the matter?' She was pushed away as he stood up.

She looked where he was pointing. Behind the sofa was a rather shabby canvas bag. Spilling out of it was a shaving set, shaving cream and two pairs of men's underpants. Alongside it was Bas's guitar. Danny looked down at her. She felt the pain in his eyes, as he once more felt threatened and uncertain. She took his hand. His fingers did not respond. 'Danny, I thought you wanted to stay with me.'

'I do. God help me I do. But Susanna—never in a million years are those—things—yours. Who is he? How long has he lived here? I have to speak to him, Susanna—face to face.'

'Maybe you should.' She looked down, meekly. She heard Bas's footsteps coming lightly up the stairs. She heard his key in the lock . . .

Danny's body tensed beside her. And then the door of the lounge was opened, and Sebastian came in. He surveyed them both with a swift glance of understanding. 'Hello Sue. Hi Dad. I've brought the lemonade.' Then he stopped. Susanna held her breath as he faced his father. Sebastian's chin wobbled just once. Then he said, his voice a little husky, 'I hope you like chow mein, Dad. It's the only thing I do that's worth eating.'

She saw Danny's eyes suddenly brimming. To help him over the moment, she said, 'I can recommend my chef. He's very good with prawns.'

Sebastian said, looking down at the two bottles of lemonade he still held, 'It looks as though you two need more than this. Shall I go out for some champagne?'

Danny cleared his throat. Then he said, 'Who needs champagne? Lemonade will be perfect.'

'Great. I'll bung this in the fridge, then.' And he went off to the kitchen. As Susanna pulled Danny towards her, Sebastian turned suddenly, 'By the way, I won't be back tonight. A late gig in Changi. I'll be staying with Ma for the rest of the week.'

'Oh but Bas—' Susanna didn't want to lose him so quickly.

Danny pulled her quickly into his arms. And as Bas winked and went back to his cooking, Danny whispered, 'Well, he is old enough to look after himself. That's what you told me anyway.'

'But—'

He bent and kissed her softly. 'We'll talk about it tomorrow. And the next day.' And she wound her arms round his neck, played lightly with the brown curls on his nape. Tonight was theirs. Tomorrow was theirs. The world was theirs.

MAY 1986 HARDBACK TITLES

——— ROMANCE ———

Surrender, My Heart *Lindsay Armstrong*	2532	0 263 11092 3
A Willing Surrender *Robyn Donald*	2533	0 263 11093 1
Prisoner *Vanessa James*	2534	0 263 11094 X
Tempest in the Tropics *Roumelia Lane*	2535	0 263 11095 8
Escape from the Harem *Mary Lyons*	2536	0 263 11096 6
The Olive Grove *Jean S. MacLeod*	2537	0 263 11097 4
Peak of the Furnace *Wynne May*	2538	0 263 11098 2
Capture a Shadow *Leigh Michaels*	2539	0 263 11099 0
Glass Slippers and Unicorns *C. Mortimer*	2540	0 263 11100 8
Wild for to Hold *Annabel Murray*	2541	0 263 11101 6
The Waiting Man *Jeneth Murrey*	2542	0 263 11102 4
Two Weeks to Remember *Betty Neels*	2543	0 263 11103 2
The Lonely Season *Susan Napier*	2544	0 263 11104 0
Bodycheck *Elizabeth Oldfield*	2545	0 263 11105 9
Win or Lose *Kay Thorpe*	2546	0 263 11106 7
Shadow Princess *Sophie Weston*	2547	0 263 11107 5

HISTORICAL ROMANCE

Where the Heart Leads *Valentina Luellen*	M143	0 263 11159 8
Fortune's Kiss *Barbara Cooper*	M144	0 263 11160 1

DOCTOR NURSE ROMANCE

Surgeon in Retreat *Jennifer Eden*	D61	0 263 11161 X
The Pagoda Doctors *Jenny Ashe*	D62	0 263 11162 8

LARGE PRINT

Dark Paradise *Sara Craven*	109	0 263 11115 6
A Durable Fire *Robyn Donald*	110	0 263 11116 4
Imperfect Chaperone *Catherine George*	111	0 263 11117 2

JUNE 1986 HARDBACK TITLES

─── ROMANCE ───

Ishbel's Party *Stacy Absalom*	2548	0 263 11125 3
Caprice *Amanda Carpenter*	2549	0 263 11126 1
Indian Silk *Joyce Dingwell*	2550	0 263 11127 X
Ride a Wild Horse *Jane Donnelly*	2551	0 263 11128 8
Adam's Law *Claudia Jameson*	2552	0 263 11129 6
Research into Marriage *Penny Jordan*	2553	0 263 11130 X
Impact *Madeleine Ker*	2554	0 263 11131 8
O'Hara's Legacy *Leigh Michaels*	2555	0 263 11132 6
Hawk's Prey *Carole Mortimer*	2556	0 263 11133 4
Never Touch a Tiger *Sue Peters*	2557	0 263 11134 2
Unlikely Lovers *Emily Spenser*	2558	0 263 11135 0
Time for Another Dream *K. van der Zee*	2559	0 263 11136 9
First Man *Kate Walker*	2560	0 263 11137 7
Innocent in Eden *Margaret Way*	2561	0 263 11138 5
The Darker Side of Loving *Yvonne Whittal*	2562	0 263 11139 3
Perfumes of Arabia *Sara Wood*	2563	0 263 11140 7

MASQUERADE HISTORICAL ROMANCE

The Garden of the Azure Dragon *Ann Hulme*	M145	0 263 11163 6
Buccaneer Bride *Kate Buchan*	M146	0 263 11164 4

DOCTOR NURSE ROMANCE

Olympic Surgeon *Margaret Barker*	D63	0 263 11167 9
The Heart Specialist *Hazel Fisher*	D64	0 263 11168 7

LARGE PRINT

Second Chance at Love *Zara Holman*	112	0 263 11118 0
The Inheritance *Kay Thorpe*	113	0 263 11119 9
By Love Bewitched *Violet Winspear*	114	0 263 11120 2